LOVE ME LIKE VOODOO

A MALVEAUX CURSE MYSTERY (BOOK 7)

G.A. CHASE

BAYOU MOON PRESS, LLC

Copyright © 2018 by G.A. Chase

First Edition 2018

Cover Art by Janet Holmes

Editing by Red Adept

ISBN eBook: 978-1-940299-55-6

ISBN print: 978-1-940299-56-3

This book is a work of fiction. Names, characters, places, and incidents are products of the author's imagination or are used fictitiously. Any resemblance to actual events, locals, business establishments, or persons, living or dead, are entirely coincidental.

Bayou Moon Press, LLC

ABOUT THIS BOOK

Love Me Like Voodoo Blurb

This the final book of the Malveuax Mystery. The grand finale where all is revealed.

While Sanguine is locked in hell, keeping an eye on the devil, Kendell and Myles are happy to finally get on with their lives. But Colin Malveaux has other plans. The devil will go to any lengths to get his deceased daughter back, even if it means ripping the fabric of multiple dimensions with her resurrection.

Now there's a bigger problem. If the divide between the living, the dead, and the damned is breached, Colin will gain command of every person's soul. As the protectors of humanity, the loas of the dead are willing to engage in all-out war to block him from taking his plan any further.

For Kendell and Myles to save the girl, stop Colin from

becoming all-powerful, and prevent the coming apocalypse, they must engage in an act of interdimensional terrorism. They'll need everyone they love to help them break the Malveaux curse and free the world of the devil.

olin Malveaux ran his hands over the polished mahogany desktop in his office at New Orleans Bank and Trust. He felt a renewed confidence. As Bank President Baron Malveaux, he'd used the desk as his command post, where he'd ruled New Orleans through loans, intimidation, and ruthless business practices. Even that paled in comparison to the role the bank desk had served after his death, when it had been his seat of power over the seventh gate to Guinee. Most recently, however, Kendell and Sanguine and their gang of fools had turned his beloved office into the fourth gate between the life he remembered and the hell they'd created for his incarceration. The elegant room had become more of a one-man prison than a palace befitting a man who had so much authority over others—and his cherished desk stood in mockery of his once-great power.

More recently, having successfully tricked his jailors

into believing he was ignorant of their little game, he was once again in charge of his destiny. *How much of an idiot did they think I was?*

Not that their foolishness regarding his understanding of hell mattered. Even if they had figured out what he knew about their seven gates, they would have simply assumed he was trying to sneak back into the land of the living. Telling Sanguine of his plan to populate hell with the souls from Guinee probably wasn't the smartest move, but it was a risk worth taking to gain her trust. Revealing a partial truth ensured he had her full confidence, and that gave him space to operate. With any luck, he might still entice her to his side.

He pulled the two pastel drawings Fleurentine Laurette-Malveaux had made of their children out of the top drawer of his desk. Even after one hundred years, Serephine's expression, captured in chalk on parchment, still touched his heart. He picked up the second drawing of her and her brother Antoine. The boy had been a roadblock to Baron Malveaux practically from the moment he was conceived. Fleur had lost her youthful waif-from-the-street sex appeal during her pregnancy. When she gave birth, the last vestige of the baron's interest for her had evaporated.

Colin pulled the scissors from his desk and cut the drawing in two. He didn't need Antoine butting in. With only the images of Serephine on his desk, Colin took the cursed pipe tool from his pocket—the same object that she'd used to kill herself.

Like a skilled jeweler preparing for a delicate watch repair, he placed the small tube of connected tools on a fresh sheet of paper along with a magnifying glass and set of microscrewdrivers. With the aid of his desk lamp, he inspected the miniature screw and flange that allowed the pipe tool to open. As he took it apart, he watched for even the tiniest of flecks to fall from the gold assembly. The tiny screw proved to be his ultimate prize. It was still coated with a brown crust. He brushed the caked blood onto the paper, being careful to not lose a single mote of dust.

He bent the white paper into a V, causing the dried blood to collect in the center, then repeated the action in the opposite direction to consolidate the flecks into small mound. The total amount of his daughter's precious essence barely covered his fingertip. He put the treasured powder to the tip of his tongue. At first it tasted like metallic dirt, but as his saliva resuscitated the girl's life force, he picked up the savory aroma of humanity.

Serephine materialized in the chair opposite him. "What am I doing here?" She sounded less scared than confused.

He touched his finger to his tongue in order to retrieve her rehydrated blood. "I called you back to save you, my darling daughter."

"But where's Baron Samedi and Antoine?" At seven years old, she still had the innocent trust that tugged at his heart.

"We don't need them any longer. Baron Samedi's only job was to guard the fourth gate, but you and your brother set me free. After that, he no longer needed to watch over you from this room. As for your brother, I'm not ready to confront him just yet. Today is just about you and me." He tried to keep his excitement from getting the better of him. Samedi had been a fool for allowing the children into

Colin's office, but the loa of the dead hadn't been the real challenge. There would still be a day of reckoning with Antoine, and if Colin's plan worked, that confrontation would be sooner rather than later.

The little girl kicked her feet back and forth under the chair. "I'm not supposed to leave Guinee alone."

"I know. After I died, I spent an eternity searching for you. I assumed you passed into the *deep waters*, but you didn't, did you?"

"I don't know anything about the *deep waters*. Did I do something wrong, Papa?"

"Nothing at all, my child. Your death was an accident. No one should have ever condemned you for a simple mistake. The loas of the dead took you from me. I now understand why I couldn't find you. It's because you didn't stay under their control. I brought you forward to this time in order to rescue you. Come to me, Serephine." He reached out his arms, hoping she would run into his embrace.

She remained in the chair. "Antoine says I shouldn't trust you."

Damn that kid. "Is he talking to you now?"

She looked down at her feet the way he remembered her doing when she'd been caught in a lie. "No, but he always looks out for me."

Colin resisted the urge to demand the hug. He needed her trust, not her fear. "I know he does. You two did agree to let me go through your gate, though. That has to count for something. I can't be all bad."

She looked up at him. "What do you want from me?"

Her trusting blue eyes made it impossible to lie to her. "I

want to save you. Your death was my fault, but I've been working really hard on fixing that mistake. You don't have to be dead any longer, Serephine. I have a replacement body ready for you. You will be the first person who can live forever. All you need to do is let me hug you."

Even in life, she'd never worried about why some things were possible and others weren't. The idea that her father, who was flesh and bone, might not be able to embrace a girl who was only spirit didn't stop her from getting off the chair and walking into his arms. She felt like sparks of electricity against his cheek and hands. He held the finger with her blood away from her spirit until he knew he had her complete love. As his hand swept through her body, the power of her soul switched from gentle shocks to a lightning bolt of searing flame. When he opened his eyes, she had vanished.

Sanguine Delarosa spread her angel wings and glided into New Orleans from her beloved swamp. The time aloft gave her the peace and privacy to consider what to do about Colin. Allowing him to have sex with her seemed like the kind of thing most religions would frown on. The question was, as an angel in this realm, how did she feel about making love with the devil?

Emotions aside, as she envisioned the mechanics of rubbing their naked bodies together with her ten-foot wingspan, she could see she would maintain a position of sexual dominance during the act. It wasn't as though she could take the submissive role of lying under him, and her wings wouldn't just stay folded up. They had a way of betraying her every emotion. *I guess faking it is out.*

Kendell and Myles would probably object to the liaison, but now that they had all but abdicated their roles in guarding Colin, Sanguine was free to do as she chose. Her body quivered in midair as if she'd hit a pocket of turbulence, but from the goose bumps on her arms, she knew the disturbance was more emotional than physical.

Far below her was a school of agitated fish in churning water. "Damn it. What is he up to this time?"

She folded her wings to her body and dove down to the wave crests. Her animal spies only caught on to Colin's activities about half of the time, and often when they were watching, he wasn't doing anything noteworthy. But as the fish kept their eyes out for any activity around the World Trade Center's paranormal vault stashed in the shipwreck, Sanguine took anything they saw as worthy of investigation.

"He wouldn't have taken Kendell again. Even he isn't that stupid. And with her safe, he doesn't have access to anyone else. He's probably just looking for a quiet place to sulk where I can't see him. It would be just like him to turn that iron interdimensional cage into a man cave."

She drifted off to the right side of the river then banked in a lazy half circle across the water. A flock of seagulls were squawking their lungs out over the trees that hid the partially submerged boat. She dove so low she was able to stare straight into the windows. At the last second, she spread her wings and gracefully set her bare feet in the three inches of water that covered the deck. *Let's see what you've been up to.*

The cabin of the luxury yacht was much the way she'd left it: walls scorched, doorframe chopped by her sword, and windows blown out. Sanguine ran her hand over the damage. "I guess we'll need to fight in less incendiary locations."

She pulled open the iron door to the vault. Inside the room, the contents had been yanked off the shelves and tossed around as if an angry adolescent had been grounded for a week in the small space. Baron Malveaux's old chests, filled with men's jewelry, desk items, and other paraphernalia cursed by Marie Laveau, lay broken on the floor. From the look of the splintered wood, it appeared some chests had been launched at the solid metal walls with considerable force.

"This damage isn't from Kendell. Colin only had her soul imprisoned, not her body. She couldn't have interacted with the boxes." Sanguine picked up one of the shattered containers and looked for teeth marks. "The dogs didn't do this either. So who did he trap this time? And what happened to them?"

Leaving the small pilothouse, she looked up at the birds for an answer. They'd already flown well inland but were still making such a racket that they couldn't be missed. She jumped into the air and flew after them with all the speed her wings could manage. She unsheathed the small dagger that responded to her anger. As she held it aloft, it lengthened to the sword she remembered, complete with rippling flames that spread from the tip to the hilt.

At the edge of the grove of trees, she saw the birds swirling around as if caught in a tornado. Below them, Colin stood on the street, looking around as if lost.

She alighted in front of him with her sword of truth still ablaze. "What have you done now?"

"None of your business." He tried walking past her as if she were just some random person on the street, but she angled the blade of fire to block his path.

"Don't make me burn you with my sword again. You don't really want another pyrotechnic argument. I might not be as able to control my anger this time. Who have you imprisoned?"

"I haven't imprisoned anyone."

His games weren't boding well for their continued relationship.

"Something tells me you're lying," she said. "You do remember you're supposed to be regaining my trust, right?"

He finally stopped looking everywhere except at her. "I was running an experiment. Unfortunately, my test subject ran off before I found out if my idea worked. At worst, I may have hurt one of your voodoo puppets."

Sanguine knew when she was hearing at least a partial truth. The flame of her sword diminished to glowing steel. "This is about your plan to save people's souls from Guinee, isn't it? What's the point? You don't have the cane back." She resisted adding *yet* to her comment.

"There are still tests I can run without it. I don't want to end up with a faulty connection. As I'm sure you'd tell me, the marionettes projected from life aren't meant to house human souls. Even you must see that a certain amount of testing would be prudent."

She returned her sword to its scabbard. "I can help you look."

The relief on his face was way too revealing. He'd done more than simply steal a virtual-reality projection. "No need, but if you're free tonight, I would enjoy taking you out to dinner. Now that you're not hiding behind that sexbot, it might be nice to get to know each other in person."

You are far too sly for your own good. "As I explained before, there's no promise of sex just because we share a meal."

"Brennan's at seven?"

She still wasn't convinced he wasn't up to something sinister, but having revealed her true self, she couldn't exactly keep following him without being noticed. Her animals would have to do. "I'll meet you there." She spread her wings. "These things don't fit comfortably in back seats."

LIKE THE RANDOM beeping of a smoke detector when the battery was dying, Myles Garrison couldn't identify the source of his irritation—only that it was somewhere in the apartment. "Why do these things always happen at three in the morning?"

Kendell Summer rolled over and kicked him under the covers. "I don't hear anything. Now, let me sleep."

"You honestly don't hear that random knocking?"

It shouldn't have surprised him. She could sleep through a hurricane.

"It's probably the neighbors," she said.

"We live on the top floor, and there's a brick wall between us and the next building. Our only real neighbors are downstairs."

She pulled the covers up over her head. "Why are you bothering me?" Her words were muffled by the thick blankets. Even their two dogs at the foot of the bed started growling at being disturbed.

For the sake of family unity, Myles got out of bed and threw on a bathrobe. "If this ends up being a Halloween skeleton that you left plugged in, you're going to owe me big time." Cheesecake, Kendell's longtime canine companion, quickly took the warm section of bed Myles had vacated.

Kendell's response was a half mumble that ended in a soft snore. Reluctantly, Doughnut Hole got off the bed to join Myles in a search of the apartment.

Myles reached down and rubbed the black Lhasa apso puppy's head. "At least I've got you watching my back."

The full moon lit up the living room, but the creepy feeling that forced Myles to check behind each chair made him search along the wall for the light switch. "I don't see anything out of the ordinary, but something's wrong. I can feel it."

Doughnut Hole looked up at him then walked to the hall closet that Myles used for his stuff. The pup lay down at the folding doors as if to prevent Myles from checking inside.

"Of course, it's that damn cane." He had to lift the dog out of the way. Behind his dress shirts and coats was the gun case he did his best to avoid. Once he had the door open, he saw the glow of the green stone that nestled under the silver skull handle. He snatched the magical staff out of the closet and headed for the veranda. On his way, he grabbed a couple of glasses and the bottle of rum he kept reserved for the loas of the dead.

He took a shot of rum to combat the outdoor chill. The cane continued to vibrate in his hand like a cell phone demanding to be answered. He set it against one of the metal chairs and filled the two glasses with rum. "Okay, I'm here. What do you want?" He hoped the conversation wouldn't last so long he'd need to take a seat, but when Papa Ghede materialized next to the cane, Myles knew it was serious. The head loa only showed up when there was bad news.

The chief of Guinee downed the glass of rum in one shot. "It's time for you to get to work."

Myles had never applied for the job of assistant to the loas of the dead, but that didn't appear to matter. Once they'd given him Baron Samedi's cane, they seemed to think he was at their beck and call.

In spite of his irritation, he sat opposite the old man. "What's the problem this time?"

The dark man helped himself to another glass of rum. "I gave you that cane for a couple of reasons. We needed it out of Guinee, in the hands of someone who wouldn't turn it over to Colin Malveaux and who serves as an ally in life we could trust. What I didn't tell you is we've had a hundred-year-old mystery that we were hoping might solve itself, and if it didn't, we had you as our backup plan. Serephine

Malveaux wasn't just killed by the curse—she was abducted from our world."

Myles balled his fists under the table. "Colin stole her soul the way he took Kendell, didn't he?"

"It's worse than that. He took her from the past. The seven gates between life and hell are your responsibility, but as Baron Samedi helped create the portals for you, we've been able to keep tabs on what was happening in hell. When Colin made it through the fourth gate, Baron Samedi's obligation to watch over Serephine and Antoine was fulfilled. Our emissary wasn't allowed to loiter around to see what happened next, so we're down to guesswork on our end."

And guessing isn't something you're good at. "If she died over a hundred years ago, and she's been missing all that time, how do you know he took her?"

"As you know, time doesn't pass for us the way you experience it. Though we knew she'd gone missing, until she was actually abducted, we couldn't tell what had happened. Colin was granted passage through the fourth gate, but he didn't move past it. As Baron Samedi was fading out of hell, he saw Colin put the drawing Serephine had given him back in his desk."

Myles had used the cane in a similar fashion to hold the door open between Guinee and hell while Kendell conducted her rescue of Sanguine. "He blocked the gate open? Then he clearly knows what we're up to."

"Again, this is speculation on our part. Even if he did keep the passage open, he would have needed a way to draw

Serephine out of Guinee and into hell. Without the cane, Colin couldn't make the trip on his own."

"He pulled Kendell through by using the curse," Myles said, "but she was directly connected to it. I can't imagine how he'd do that with the young girl."

"Whatever his method, Serephine's soul doesn't belong in hell. We can't redeem her without entering Colin's realm. But by invading another dimension, we would create a rift between worlds that would be hard to contain."

Cheesecake walked up to Papa Ghede's chair and started growling.

"It's okay, girl." Kendell walked out of the living room and wrapped the blanket from the bed tightly around her before sitting next to Myles. "Tell me what happened when Serephine was taken a hundred years ago. How could you not have known what happened back then?"

"Think of it as an IOU for her soul. From our historic perspective, we knew at some point in the future Baron Samedi would vouch for the request. He did that when you asked Serephine to act as gate guardian for your fourth gate. Until we passed the date, however, we couldn't know what would happen."

Kendell lifted Cheesecake to her lap to stop the dog's growling. "So even though Colin was allowed to pass the fourth gate, because he didn't go through, Serephine never returned to Guinee? What about Antoine?"

Figuring out purgatory's relationship to time gave Myles a headache. "He was just a boy when we saw him at the fourth gate, but we know he lived to be an old man. Was he even from Guinee's dimension, or had he passed on the *deep waters?*"

Papa Ghede toyed with the glass as though he wanted another drink but dared not risk getting intoxicated. "People can be whatever age they want while they're in Guinee, up until the age of their death. To simplify their discussion with their father, Antoine decided to be an age appropriate to when his sister had died. The IOU is still outstanding for him. At this moment, his soul is caught between dimensions. Until the IOU is fulfilled, or not, we can't see what ultimately happed to his soul."

Kendell snuggled the furry dog tightly to her chest. "Sounds like what I went through while trapped in Colin's vault. At least Antoine is safe."

Myles put his arm around Kendell to hold her close. "If Serephine isn't still in the bank, she might be experiencing what happened to you when you got out of that cage."

Papa Ghede finally poured himself another glass of rum. "And this is why we need your help. If Colin did steal her soul and let her out of the fourth gate, she'd be in her own personal demonic nightmare. We loas of the dead take our responsibility for all human spirits very personally. We are willing to risk an interdimensional war rather than lose a single human being, but using you to find her would prevent such a conflict. Some fires are hard to extinguish once they're lit."

Myles took the cane from the chair. "So Kendell and I cross into hell and save her. How exactly do we do that?"

Papa Ghede downed the last of his drink. "Life and hell are your dimensions. I gave you the cane as a form of travel, but figuring out the map is your problem. Just don't take the route through Guinee again. I know it may seem like the most obvious path, but after what Colin's done, we're working on a permanent closing of that rift. If you were to rely on that opening, you might end up trapped on the wrong side."

---

2

*C*olin knew Sanguine wouldn't leave him alone for long. With little else to do in hell—and him as the only other living being—she might turn her back on him for the afternoon if he was lucky. Even then, every animal he encountered, other than his squadron of mosquitoes, could easily be reporting back to their swamp-witch mistress.

"Where would my daughter go?" He needed to find the child before Sanguine stumbled across her.

He retraced his steps from the river to the bank with little optimism. Though the old building had been the fourth gate Serephine had presided over, it had also been her access from Guinee when Colin had rescued her from the loas' tyranny. Returning to the scene of what they considered a crime would be a risk. Still, as the location of her most recent memories, she might use it as a starting point.

Though he searched the streets for any sign of the lost

child during his walk, all he saw was the usual parade of puppets carrying out their scripted movements. Based on the chaos Serephine had created in the vault, he imagined there would be a swath of destruction behind her like the trail of debris left by a miniature tornado. "If you'd have only waited for me, I could have helped you adjust. Why did you run?"

As expected, on entering the bank, there was no little girl sitting at his desk. He examined the carved wooden mural of the city that took up every inch of wainscoting. The old family mansion on Saint Charles Avenue had been torn down not long after Baron Malveaux's death.

"Would you have known that our old home was destroyed?"

Even if she had braved walking to the Garden District, chasing her all over the city seemed like a waste of his time. He needed to figure out where she'd end up.

He pulled out his cell phone. "I need the town car. We're headed to the Laurette mansion."

Though Antoine's crowning architectural achievement had been badly burned, Serephine had always gravitated to her brother in times of trouble. At least it was a place to start.

As he left the bank, he looked to the sky. With her wings, Sanguine could fly over the neighborhoods like a guardian angel, searching for the girl. He felt bad about lying to the mysterious woman, and not just because he could really use her help. *Has it really only been days since you showed up in your angelic state, revealing your true self to me?* Her fit of raw anger had been almost as revealing as her wings. No one bothered to engage in that intense of an argument if they didn't care. She could have run him through with her sword and been done with him permanently, but she hadn't.

Colin turned back to the street as he heard the car pull up. He peered through the driver's window without waiting for the man to come around and open the back door. "We're going to be exploring the city. I need to find that child's body you helped me abduct, so keep your eyes open while you're driving."

Once he was in the back seat, Colin swung round to every window, hoping for some sign of the girl. After passing the hotel that occupied the location of the old family estate, the driver turned the car into the residential neighborhood of the Garden District. Colin had the driver creep the long vehicle down the potholed streets, but nothing looked out of place. Even the dilapidated Laurette mansion appeared undisturbed.

He tapped on the back of the driver's seat. "Stop here. Even if she's not in the gutted building, I won't rest easy unless I go in and see for myself."

The man remained behind the wheel like a robot waiting for its next command.

Why do I even bother? Colin got out of the car and headed up the walkway as though walking into a dreaded family reunion. He'd purchased the derelict building with the intention of rebuilding it to its past glory. What the baron's son could build, Colin could improve on. But that had been as Lincoln Laroque. The up-and-coming businessman had still had unresolved issues regarding gaining his family's respect. Colin shook his head at the foolishness. *If two heads are better than one, two lifetimes make a path even clearer.*

He pushed open the warped door and walked into the foyer that still smelled of smoke. The handmade reproduction green-and-yellow-flowered wallpaper was now shades of black and gray. The once-cheerful blooms reminded him of wilted bouquets.

"Serephine, are you in here?"

Though he'd hoped for an answer, he wasn't surprised to hear nothing but the silent ghosts from the past.

"If you didn't make it into the body I prepared for you, know that I'm still trying to save you. Find a way to reach me."

He struggled to slide open the pocket doors to the study Anthony Laurette had used as his architectural office. The wall behind the substantial oak desk had been salvaged from the Malveaux mansion. Colin ran his hands over the carved edges of the grand bookcase, remembering when it had graced his den in the old estate. "I'm surprised you saved this. I wonder if it was some remembrance of me, or simply the appreciation of fine craftsmanship."

"Neither."

Colin swung around and saw Anthony Laurette standing in the doorway.

"I kept that garish wall as a reminder not to become you and as a memorial to Sere," Anthony said. "She killed herself in front of that cabinet. Now, what have you done with my sister?"

Colin pulled the chair out from the desk and took a seat. The move was meant to put Anthony in his place, but if the baron's son took offense, he didn't show it. "Did the loas of the dead send you?"

"No one sent me. *You* were the one who trapped me in the fourth gate by not removing the drawing. Now, I'll ask you again: what have you done with my sister?" With his Confederate officer's uniform, long scraggly beard, and sword wound that traversed his face, Anthony was far from the innocent teenager Colin remembered from the bank office.

I must remember to burn that damn drawing next time I'm in the bank. That should either send him back to Guinee or trap him between dimensions. Either way, he'll no longer be a thorn in my side. "Serephine is going through a transformation. When I'm done, she will be immortal."

"You mean forever trapped under your bootheel."

Colin had never dealt with his son after the war. The boy had really become a man, and one not easily manipulated. "Why is it that no one can accept my love for Serephine? I'm not out to hurt her. What I do is for the overall good of humanity."

"I've heard you make similar comments regarding defeated adversaries. You've spoken that way too many times for me to believe in some ultimate goodness you believe you possess. Sere is trapped between dimensions. You've turned her into a monster. Nothing you do will change what you've created inside that innocent child. Even if by some miracle she does survive this transformation of yours, you'll never understand the new darkness that will forever inhabit her soul. You truly are the devil."

Colin couldn't even entertain the idea that Serephine

would come back as anything other than his beloved daughter. "I haven't finished saving her. Once I find her, I can solve whatever problem she's encountered. If you know where she is, you'd be doing her a favor in telling me."

"You don't even know what's become of her, do you? I can't help you. I'm merely the reflection of a memory. The loas allowed me these brief connections with you in the hope that I could get you to see the truth of your plan. Taking the souls entrusted to their care and creating a new living world order will result in demons. Instead of people connecting with each other, every human will be out for themselves—an unending battle to reach the top of the ladder without even death as a comfort."

The explanation sounded scripted, as if Anthony were reading from the loas' playbook.

"I'll take my chances. Anything would beat the reality that Papa Ghede created."

"You don't really care about Sere at all, do you?" Anthony asked.

"She's stronger than you think. She's *my* daughter. After all of the dimensional transfers I've endured, I know a thing or two about survival. Serephine will lead the way for all of humanity. Without the evil that people see in me, she'll be the one to fully create what I have envisioned."

Anthony's body became translucent. "Just do me the favor of *not* bringing me back from the dead. I'd prefer to rest in peace rather than face an eternity at war. I've already served my time."

Colin stormed out to the town car with a renewed disdain for his son.

"Where to next, Boss?"

He checked his watch. "Better take me back to the condo. I need to get ready for dinner."

~

SANGUINE'S WINGS quivered as she opened the door to Brennan's restaurant. Self-consciousness was seldom an issue for her, but walking into the fancy establishment where the customers dressed nearly as elegantly as the waiters had her checking her goddess dress for stray cypress needles. She folded her wings tightly behind her to avoid knocking over any crystal stemware on the tables as she was guided to her seat.

Colin got up as she approached. "You look lovely this evening. I've been looking forward to dining with the real you since you first revealed your true self."

She spread her wings to the sides of the chair and blocked out the rest of the dining room. "I'm feeling a little out of place."

"An angel deserves to be treated like royalty."

His flattery got on her nerves. Even though she knew better, she examined the potential futures the evening might create. No matter which choice of conversation she picked, she didn't see them making it past the main course before breaking out into a fight. She hoped to avoid the scenario in which she drew her flaming sword and lit the linen tablecloth on fire.

Remember, swing from above, not below. "What's good to eat here?"

"I'm particularly fond of the duck, but everything is superb."

She resisted looking at him to see if he was checking out her wings after the duck comment. *Everything looks so wonderful. It's a shame we won't be getting to the main course. I guess there's no point in putting this off.* She closed her menu and set it in front of her. "As you know, I have some ability to see the future, but only up to the next decision point. For example, I know we're about to have a fight, but I don't know about what. Beyond that argument, I don't know what happens. So you might as well tell me why I'm about to be mad at you."

He carefully set his menu on the table as if any sudden movement might set off an explosion. "I need your help."

She consulted her future visions again in the hope that she'd missed something. "I hadn't expected you to need anything."

He waved to the waiter. "Bring us a couple of whiskeys. Make them doubles."

Even without consulting her future sight, she could imagine her flaming sword igniting the alcohol. "I'm not sure that's such a good idea."

"Strong alcohol on a date never is, but as you suspected, this night probably won't end up with us snuggled in bed—though I confess I'm really curious how you'd handle sex with those wings. I might be developing an angel fetish."

The waiter set the glasses on the table as if Sanguine and Colin were about to start a competition to see who could drink more.

Sanguine took a sip of the whiskey to calm her nerves.

"Out with it." The sword at her side was already warming up.

"Have you had any further thoughts about my idea of saving souls from Guinee?"

You are really getting on my nerves with these delaying tactics. She tried to keep her cool for as long as possible. "If you're asking if I talked to Myles about his cane, I have."

"I'm not asking about specifics. Without you by my side, my plan will be much more complicated. What I'm really interested in tonight is how you're feeling about being my partner in this endeavor."

Are my foolish unrequited romantic desires really why I'm going to get pissed off? "I thought we were on a date, not a business meeting."

"I would like nothing better than to enjoy a fine meal with you while we get to know each other better, but I do have a pressing problem. How you feel about working with me will determine how I explain my situation."

She could see that the battle scene had been delayed at least until they finished their drinks. "I think I might be willing to risk the shrimp ravigote appetizer."

"I'll take that as progress." He motioned to the waiter, who never seemed more than a discreet distance from the table. The man had the good sense to take the order and not hang around to offer advice about the menu.

"If we survive the night," she said, "one thing that would be worth knowing about me is that I'm very direct. Playing around the outskirts of a topic seldom results in an easier conversation."

He smiled at her over the rim of his whiskey glass. "We

have that in common. Very well. I didn't lie to you earlier today, but my experiment was more involved than I let on. Even without the cane, I've been able to contact another soul and entice them to this realm."

She couldn't tell if the sizzling sound was from her sword setting fire to the tablecloth or the bananas foster being served at the next table. "You stole another soul?" She did her best not to yell, but the attempt at control made every word sound like an indictment.

"I wouldn't do that. Technically, I'm still the girl's guardian."

Sanguine rested her hand on the hilt of her sword, ready to draw it even if the action did create a scene. "Justifications and fudging the truth are just other means of being indirect."

He leaned back in his chair and raised his hands as if expecting her to throw her drink at him. "I met Serephine at the fourth gate between life and hell. She accepted my confession. Since you would only consider my explanation of the specifics as delaying the truth, here are the basic facts. I brought her soul out of Guinee and placed it in one of the virtual people you have running around in this world. I meant to catch up with Serephine at the vault, but the vault was already open when I got there. I don't know if the transfer worked or if the human robot managed to break free before I could put Serephine's soul into the body. I've spent the afternoon searching every place I can think of where my daughter might go, but I haven't found even a clue as to her whereabouts."

The blade burned so hot Sanguine could feel it scorching

her leg. A part of her argued, however, that Colin was simply trying to save his daughter, who'd succumbed to the curse that was the result of his actions. *I need to avoid this fight in order to save the child.* "So you either have a scared, confused, and lost little girl wandering the streets of New Orleans, or you have a virtual projection that will return to its normal life and the ghost of your daughter who you'll never find."

"Hearing you say it makes me wonder why I came here tonight. A good father would still be out there searching."

She enjoyed her whiskey while watching him squirm. "No one is ever going to consider you a good father, but I can appreciate your willingness to ask for my help. That couldn't have been easy. Where have you searched so far?"

"Mostly the Garden District. That's where Baron Malveaux lived and later where his son—as Anthony Laurette—built his mansion. I thought she might try to find one of the old houses."

Sanguine took her time with the plate of shrimp. "You are such a fool. Children don't run to places. They run to people they know. Having escaped you and knowing her brother was still in Guinee, she would have struck out in search of her mother. Though the nuns are done with the rest of us, they'd never turn their backs on a lost child."

He dabbed at his mouth with his napkin. She thought he was going to put it on the table and request that they leave for the convent immediately, but he only said, "If we're going to stay through the meal, I'm going to need more whiskey."

"Make it a single for me. We can go once we finish our

appetizers. There's no point in rushing, as the nuns probably won't let us in even if Serephine did end up over there."

Colin settled back in his chair. "Thank you for doing this."

"Don't get any foolish ideas. I'm not doing this out of love for you. Kendell was the driving force behind the seven gates that hold you prisoner in hell. Since my grandmother turned this realm over to me, I suppose that makes me the warden. Serephine is an innocent victim of your evil doings. I won't be responsible for her added suffering in my dimension."

He grabbed the whiskey from the waiter and took a drink before the man had an opportunity to put it on the table. "What do I have to do to win you over?"

"Are you asking romantically or professionally? Even though you've unburdened your soul about Serephine, I'm still unclear if this is supposed to be a date or a business dinner."

He set his half-finished drink on the table. "Would you entertain the possibility that my intentions are both?"

"In your case? No. Either you're trying to win my heart so I'll accept your plan and follow you no matter what you wish to do, or you're trying to soften my opinion of you by showing me what a noble plan you've hatched. Either way, there is an ulterior desire, and your actions toward me are merely a means to an end."

The appetizers were nearly gone. If he planned on anything more than a walk to the convent, time was running out.

"You never have thought very much of me," he said.

Clever. Now you've got me considering your positive attributes. "I admire your cunning. Even with our team of people from varying backgrounds, we've had a hard time keeping up with your shenanigans. Each time we think you'll go right, you turn left, but we all know there's an ultimate destination out there somewhere. You've just been skilled in keeping it a secret."

"I told you my plan. Is it really so hard to believe I want to end human death?"

She was down to her last spoonful of shrimp. "But that's not your ending point. The question is, what do you do with all those people you save? In my experience, God and the devil are two sides of the same coin of dominance. Unless you intend on tossing away the dichotomy and letting people live as they wish, I have no reason to trust you."

Colin wondered if Sanguine was intentionally dragging her feet, or if having wings had somehow affected her ability to walk at a decent pace. "I know I invited you on a date, and a nice leisurely stroll after dinner is kind of romantic, but do you think you could move a little faster? We're kind of beyond the gazing-at-the-stars section of the evening."

"I just didn't want you tripping into the gutter. You downed that last whiskey pretty fast. Would you prefer that I took you in my arms and flew us to the convent?"

He winced at the idea of being so subservient to a woman. "I can walk just fine, thank you very much. I'd just rather not wake the nuns up. They tend to be grumpy enough during the day."

"You're assuming that they're even going to open their gates to us."

The nuns might not be the common enemy that would unit Colin and Sanguine, but they did provide a shared focus—and one over which he held some leverage. "They wouldn't dare keep me out after all the money I've donated."

"I guess we'll find out soon enough. If Serephine is only a ghost, the nuns might not be much help. And even if she did make it into your prepared vessel, she might not figure out where her mother ended up. She was just a child when she committed suicide. Her mother didn't enter the convent until long after Serephine had entered Guinee."

He hammered his fist against the solid-wood door of the abbey. "Stop making excuses to cover if you're wrong. I can't handle someone not standing up for their ideas, just as much as you hate indirectness."

The door to the convent opened all the way, revealing the Reverend Mother in her torn, dirty habit. "You'd better come with me."

At least the woman walked faster than Sanguine, but the buildings still weren't getting closer as quickly as Colin would have liked.

"Do you have my daughter?"

The old woman flapped her arms like Sanguine did when she was about to take flight. "We have someone who's very mixed up. As you two are the only actual beings in this realm, I have to assume one of you is responsible for this mess."

The Reverend Mother stopped at the door to the meeting room. "I won't be joining you." She opened the door and thrust Colin and Sanguine in before closing and latching it tight.

Colin thought he'd met every form of angry interdimensional being possible, but seeing Miss Fleur fly at him with eyes blazing, hair erupting like lightning, and teeth bared made her the equal of Agnes Delarosa in her hurricane.

"What have you done to our daughter?" Miss Fleur's voice rattled the stained glass windows.

Colin was in no mood to fight with another emotional female. "Is she here?"

"Every word in that question presents a new problem. *Here* would imply a single dimension. *She* is questionable in that the being we're holding is more crazed animal than human. Even *is* leaves me wondering. Haven't you done enough to Serephine? Why couldn't you let that poor, sweet, innocent soul rest in peace?"

Sanguine spread her wings. The gesture at least calmed down Fleurentine's outrage. "Can I see her?"

Colin stood next to his winged angel. "The sooner the better."

Fleurentine waved her bony finger at him. "Not you, just her. You're not going any closer to our daughter than this room where I can keep an eye on you. I must have been a fool thinking there was any vestige of the Archibald I remembered. He never would have done this to our daughter—though when she found you were so evil that she thought it necessary to kill herself over your actions, that should have been my first clue as to your true nature. I'm beginning to understand what Serephine detected in you. And I'd thought her death was about your brothels."

"If you think I'm standing here while Sanguine goes and checks on our daughter, then this place has turned your brain into mush." His anger was getting the better of him. "I can still help."

"The hell you can." Miss Fleur grabbed him by the lapel and dragged him through the long meeting hall. Sanguine flapped her wings to keep up.

At the end of the stone hallway, a balcony overlooked a sunken room lined with thin dormitory mattresses. A thick pane of glass separated the observers from the incarcerated. On the floor of the cell, a childlike animal ran on all fours as fast as she could and slammed headfirst into the padded wall. Her screams must have echoed clear up to the bell tower above, but the sound was filled less with pain than rage.

Brother Aramis emerged from the side office. "The Reverend Mother called me the minute they found this unfortunate wandering the streets. The Church used to call her affliction *being possessed*. In most of those cases, lost souls were trapped between dimensions. Exorcisms were really nothing more than an attempt at reconnecting a person to their reality. But what you've done is beyond our ability to help. There's no reality for her to connect to. Her time is wrong. Her body is not her own. And she has no business being in hell. You've truly created a monster.

All the Church and I can do is give her what peace we can."

Colin gripped the balcony railing to prevent taking a swing at the cleric. "By locking her in a dungeon?" He had never in his life wanted to resort to bodily harm more than he did at that moment.

"By reducing her stimulations to a minimum. In her condition, every movement or sound is amplified and distorted to the point that a normal human brain can't process the inputs. Of course, as she is just a child—in both body and spirit—she has even less ability to understand what's happening. Down there, she's not as subjected to the demonic hallucinations that are all too real for her."

Colin turned to Sanguine in despair. "Help her."

Sanguine leaned on the railing and spread her wings. She looked every bit the guardian angel. "I only have control of what my grandmother built. I do know of two people who have experience with this sort of thing. If you thought winning me over was a challenge, you're going to have to up your game to convince Kendell and Myles to come help."

3

"*I* suppose our first stop should be Delphine's."
Myles had never trusted the voodoo
practitioner, but he had to confess that no one knew more
about interdimensional travel than she did. The cane was
like a spaceship, and so far, he'd been little more than the
monkey strapped to the seat, pretending he understood the
controls. *Why can't someone give me a simple instruction
manual for that damn thing?*

Kendell sat on the floor of their apartment, brushing out
Cheesecake's winter fur. "Even though Papa Ghede said we
couldn't use Guinee as our portal, you don't think the loas
might simply look the other way? After all, their leader set
us on this mission. We have used the cane to walk into
Guinee before. Surely, they could put off their construction
project long enough for us to save a soul."

"Even if we did pass through Guinee, that route to hell
only works if I remain in the doorway between dimensions,

holding the portal open. I'm not standing by while you go risking your neck again. Besides, Papa Ghede said not to. If the loas do manage to seal the hole between dimensions, we really will be screwed in hell. Then there's Colin to consider. Since he has accessed the fourth gate and I'm in charge of number five, he'll be looking for me. I'm not going into hiding just so he can steal someone I love in order to force me into the open. This time, I'm facing him head-on."

Doughnut Hole gave a defiant bark of agreement, but Cheesecake looked at Kendell and whimpered.

Kendell cleaned the thick white-and-black fur from the brush. "I'm with my dog. You taking on Colin seems like a bad idea, especially while in his hell dimension."

"We're talking about a couple of steps down the road. Until we figure out how to bodily travel to hell, we're just speculating. My conflict with Colin will come to a head sooner or later. All I'm saying is if I am in hell, he'll have no reason to hold you hostage." Myles headed for the closet to grab his cane.

"I'm not up for another voodoo-totem spaceship ride between dimensions." Her voice came through clearly even though she was in a different room. The apartment was small enough that no one ever had to yell.

"That trip was purely spiritual anyway," Myles said. "The cane is the key to interdimensional travel, both metaphysical and bodily. Last time, using that totem was the only means Delphine could suggest for leading Colin on our little cat-and-mouse chase. I just need to understand how to use this staff. Then crossing dimensions should be as easy as moving from one room into the next."

"Don't you think some things are better off not known?" she asked.

He stood in the living room doorway—cane in hand and dog sitting at attention next to his leg. "You don't have to join me if you don't want to."

Her frown with head tilted was a look he knew all too well. "Of course I'm coming with you," she said. "I just thought we should look at this from all sides first."

At least you didn't say you were playing the devil's advocate. "I think the time for speculation on the best course to heal Serephine is over." Myles leaned down and petted Doughnut Hole's head. "Stay here and keep an eye on things."

As they walked the handful of blocks to the perfumery with its hidden voodoo library, Myles tried to remember everything he'd learned about crossing dimensions. "If we don't get this right, I'm worried we'll become as messed up as you were coming out of Colin's vault. It seems like we're trying to step from a waiting platform onto a train traveling at a high speed with its doors closed."

She nodded. "There are only a couple of ways to get us both into hell, but none of them seem easy. The more I think about it, the more I agree with you that sneaking through Guinee won't work. We're both going to be needed in hell, and if you're holding the gate open, we'll be shorthanded. We do have the gates from hell to life, but using those is way too dangerous. Colin stole my soul through the seventh gate, which I'm watching, and it sounds like he's pulled a similar trick in nabbing Serephine. The interdimensional embassies are only good for talking to the other side, not crossing over. And we don't have a voodoo artifact that's half in this dimension and half in the other like we did when the band drove into hell. The cane is our last resort."

Myles wondered how the simple stick in his hand could be so powerful. "Hopefully, Delphine knows more than she's let on. But then, that wouldn't be anything new."

"Be nice." Kendell pushed open the door to Scratch and Sniff.

Delphine sat behind the counter in her usual African-motif wrap. "What new voodoo nightmare have you gotten into today?"

Myles lifted the cane. "I need to understand how to use this thing. Kendell and I have to get to hell to save Serephine Malveaux."

"Of course you do." The woman's sarcastic tone made Myles consider hitting her over the head with the stick.

As always, Kendell did her best to smooth the interactions. "Papa Ghede himself has given us this mission. You know how the loas feel about losing a soul."

"It's never happened before." Delphine hung the closed sign out front before leading them to the hidden library in the back room. "I remember Marie Laveau writing something about Baron Malveaux's use of the cane to move through dimensions."

Myles remained standing, letting Kendell take the single guest chair in the small room while Delphine thumbed through her journals. "We're going to need to transport more than just one person."

"Next you're going tell me you want to take your dogs

on the journey again." Delphine set the large leather-bound ledger on the table. "Here it is. Apparently, Baron Archibald Malveaux didn't die before entering Guinee."

"What?" Kendell bolted from her chair to look at the book.

"Marie claims they never found a body. The authorities attributed his disappearance to foul play, but the case remained unsolved." Delphine looked up at Myles. "Maybe Chief of Police Laroque has more on the official answer of what happened to his ancestor, but according to Marie, he used the cane to cross over. Since he never returned, she couldn't verify her assumption."

"Great," Myles said. "Kendell and I have already walked into Guinee by using the cane, so the fact that Baron Malveaux might have done the same thing isn't exactly news—though, since he left Guinee to possess my body, I'm a little suspicious of Marie's conclusion. If I'd been alive in the late 1800s and wanted to kill that asshole, I'm pretty sure I could have made the body disappear in the swamps. And in case you've forgotten, you did imprison his soul in your little voodoo totem. Had you not done that, Lincoln Laroque wouldn't have mysteriously gotten his hands on it and drunk the baron's essence to become Colin Malveaux. Those things wouldn't be doable if Baron Malveaux were still in his own body. Sounds to me like Marie got it wrong."

"Don't get snippy with me. I'm just relaying what Marie wrote. It's not like I've had that cane to play with. Why haven't you performed one of your psychometric tricks to read its past? You must have figured something out by now

—or have you just been hiding the walking stick under your bed, hoping it won't bite you in the ass?"

"Both of you, stop," Kendell said. "We have to assume the cane needs to be taught how to do things similar to how a dog is trained. Even if Baron Malveaux did eventually die, his first crossing into Guinee might have been in bodily form. Once he crossed back, he wasn't likely to need Marie's services any longer. And as Myles said, we have used the cane to cross into the realm of the loas, so we know the staff can do that trick already. Someone had to be the first. If we assume it *was* Baron Malveaux, Colin would retain the memory of how he did it."

Myles didn't see how their enemy understanding what they had to do was any help at all. "Even better. All I need to do is hand him the cane so he can show me how it works. That should end well."

Kendell pressed her hands to the table. "Keep it up, and we won't have to figure out how to transport two people. You can make the trip on your own."

Myles knew he'd let his irritation at Delphine get the better of him. He put his hand on Kendell's back as a sign of contrition. "I'm sorry. I didn't mean to piss you off. How do you propose we get Colin to tell us what he knows?"

"Apology accepted." She stood up and took him in her arms. "We're going to need Sanguine to be present when we talk to Colin. Even if she can't get the answers out of him, she'll know when he's lying. Then we'll need a way to verify what Colin says so we don't end up back in his evil little vault."

Delphine closed the journal. "I wish I could be of more

help, but neither I nor Marie had possession of the cane. We've only been the intermediaries, and the loas don't confide in their lackeys."

Myles gripped the head of the cane. "That's at least one thing we can agree on."

As they left the shop, Kendell pulled out her cell phone.

"Who are you calling?"

"Polly and the band. It's a long drive out to the swamp."

He aimed his cane toward the far end of the Quarter. "Tell them to meet us at the club. I meant it when I said I was done avoiding Colin. We can contact—" But before he finished, he heard the familiar ringing in his ears that indicated someone was trying to access his gate in the speakeasy behind the Scratchy Dog. "Apparently, we're not the only ones who want to talk. Tell the band to hurry." He swung the cane as he walked toward Frenchmen Street.

Though he didn't mean to set a brisk pace, Kendell had to jog to keep up. "And if it is Colin on the other end of the call and he tries to pull you through the gate, what then?"

Myles lifted the cane. "If he did that even with you and the band present? Honestly, I'd like to see him try. If he did succeed, that would be one less problem to figure out."

KENDELL HATED the idea of using Myles's fifth gate as a cell phone to hell, and not just because Colin had so successfully drawn her and Serephine through their gate connections. "You do realize this is the next gate Colin needs to pass through. We could be playing right into his hands. Though it is a drive out to the swamp, at least there we're less likely to be manipulated over Sanguine's gate."

Myles was busy opening the shutters to the speakeasy while the band pulled chairs out of the club. The small courtyard looked as if it were being prepared for a ceremony. "That's why I've got you and the band with me. I'm not pouring that bastard any drinks unless we all agree. Plus, even if it is Colin who's calling, I'm counting on Sanguine being there with him."

"I still don't like it."

Myles drew the veve on the counter to indicate he was present. "Now you know how I felt every time you dove headfirst into another conflict without me."

Kendell already knew she'd put everyone she cared about through quite a lot. She walked up to Myles while he was still preparing the communication link and threw her arms around him from behind. "In each of those dangers, I knew I had you there to save me. I promise that if something does go wrong, I won't rest until I've proven to be equally strong." With the veve complete, she breathed a little easier at seeing Sanguine on the projection. "I'm glad to see it's you."

"Don't get too excited." Sanguine stood aside to show that Colin was with her. "We've got a problem on this side."

Myles set the cane under the bar where it wouldn't be noticed over the connection. "Wouldn't have anything to do with Colin stealing Serephine Malveaux's spirit out of Guinee, now, would it?"

Colin shoved his way into the center of the projection. "Those damn loas of the dead told you. Well, I'm not surprised. But I didn't *steal* anyone. Serephine came willingly. The loas of the dead were the ones holding her captive. I was only rescuing my daughter from those soul abductors."

Nice spin. You should have entered politics. Kendell chose a more diplomatic response. She didn't want to be the one to start the fight. "Tell us what happened."

Like Kendell, Sanguine took over her end of the conversation in more reasonable tones than the men were using. "Colin had an idea that he could pull a soul from Guinee and put it into one of the virtual-projection people in this realm." She looked intently at Kendell. "As you can imagine, that didn't go so well. The girl not only switched dimensions like you did, but she's also in the wrong time and body. As a seven-year-old child, she can't process the experience. She's in the convent. The nuns and Miss Fleur are doing what they can, but we need someone with a better understanding of interdimensional transfers. We don't have the first clue how to heal the child. She's more wild animal than human. No one can reach her."

Kendell shook her head. "We've already talked to Delphine. I'm afraid she wasn't much help."

"I meant you and Myles, silly. No one would understand what Serephine is going through better than you, and though Delphine might have her uses, only Myles has been able to move another person through dimensions."

Myles folded his arms and glared at Colin. "About that… from Marie Laveau's journals, it would appear that as Baron Malveaux, you managed to cross from life to Guinee with the cane. Mind sharing how you did it?"

"And you'd believe me?" Colin had the usual irascible expression on his face.

"No, but it would be a place to start if you expect our help. First, though, I want you to convince me this isn't another ploy to steal my cane. There's no point in continuing this conversation if this is just another one of your games."

Colin lowered his eyes, directing his direct glare of defiance toward the floor. "She's my daughter."

"That's not an assurance—it's another reason why you might be inclined to take the magic staff."

Kendell wanted to offer Colin some sympathy, but Myles was right. If they were going to make another trip into hell—this time to *help* Colin—they at least deserved proof this wasn't another move in his complex game of deception.

"In the time that I've known you, you've stolen my dog, my band, my lover, and my soul," she said. "You must see why we don't trust you."

Colin looked up with the familiar cold-eyed stare. "And I've been cast into hell with no one to talk to but a snarky avenging angel who on the rare occasion agrees to sleep with me using her sex dolls."

Sanguine turned to Colin. "I did warn you that you'd have your work cut out for you. Right now, even I'm reconsidering my agreement to help."

From the way Colin regulated his breathing, his effort at self-control was all too obvious. "Tell me what you want. How can I convince you this mission isn't about me? If I could step out of hell for a minute so you could save my daughter, I would."

Myles looked about to continue the argument, but Kendell took his hand. "He may be onto something. What if we sealed him in the vault for the time we're in hell?"

"It's *his* vault," Myles said. "He's already proven he can unlock it, and we can't do a damn thing with it other than opening and closing the door. I doubt even Luther Noire would be able to secure it from Colin's use."

"You've already sent me a jailor." Colin motioned to Sanguine. "Surely there must be some place in this hell where you could put me with her standing guard—maybe the World Trade Center or Saint Louis Cathedral? Consider this conversation a white flag on my part. I don't expect you to take my word of honor, but I will accept yours that once my daughter is cured, you'll let me out of whatever cell you devise."

"No way," Myles said. "We've already seen you take control of the World Trade Center from Luther Noire, and we know you manipulated Brother Aramis into giving you access to the fail-safe that released your vault. Securing you in an embassy is like locking a child in a candy store."

Sanguine crossed her arms. She flapped her wings a couple of times as if she were working out an idea. "I could take Colin out to the swamp. He wouldn't have any other means of transportation, and if he did somehow get past me and try to escape, he'd run up against my alligators. It takes me out of a position to help Serephine, but after seeing her, I'm not sure what more I could do to help. What she's suffering from is beyond my comprehension."

Myles slowly reached under the bar and pulled out the cane. His eyes never left Colin. "Just because you would be locked up doesn't mean you couldn't work up some other game to nab this cane."

Kendell also watched Colin for any reaction that might betray his true intentions. If he was still after the object, he wasn't outwardly drooling for it like a mad dog.

"I can only give you my word so many times," Colin said. "Since you won't believe me, what do you propose?"

Myles twisted the cane in his hand. "I don't have an answer, but I reserve the right to add to your restrictions should I come up with something. The next problem I see is the question of what happens to Serephine once she's cured. The loas of the dead want her soul back in Guinee where she belongs."

"Out of the question." Colin gripped the sides of the metal chair. "They took her too soon. She was just a child. I'm righting a wrong. I want her to be mentally whole again, but I'm not turning her over to those worshippers of death."

Kendell wondered if she would have reacted any differently if she had lost a child. "I think we can all agree that healing Serephine's soul is our first priority."

Myles tapped the cane against the brick-covered ground. "Papa Ghede would not agree. He sounded pretty adamant that I was to go to hell and return Serephine to Guinee by any means possible. They might not take kindly to me helping the entity they still see as Baron Malveaux—usurper of Guinee."

"I don't give a damn what those voodoo fools want." Colin's grip on the arms of his chair showed white

44

knuckles. He half rose out of his seat. "Serephine is my daughter. I'll do whatever you want to gain your help, but I will not sacrifice her soul."

Much as Kendell hated the man, she had to admire his passion for his daughter. "I don't want to get into a negotiation for her soul. I've experienced only a fraction of what Serephine is going through, and every second was an eternal damnation. We need to help her first and worry about her fate later."

Colin's smile didn't put Kendell at ease. "That would be acceptable to me."

She put her hand on Myles's back to prevent him from taking the argument with Colin any further. "So we have two shaky agreements: Colin will stay out of the way, and we'll do what we can to make Serephine whole. The big obstacle is our traveling to hell." She turned back to Colin. "What do you know about the cane?"

"The secret is in the silver handle," Colin said. "It must be removed in order to use the full power of the cane. It's like a lock preventing the cane from taking on any new programming."

MYLES SLAMMED the shutters down on the speakeasy. "I don't trust him, and I don't like the plan." He couldn't prevent the feeling that they'd all just been played. Sanguine had as much as confessed she had feelings for the devil. Colin could be a manipulative bastard when it came to women. *I should have included Charlie for an additional male*

perspective. And though Myles wanted to help Serephine, everyone was putting a lot of trust in his abilities with the cane.

Kendell helped close up the gate to hell. "I think we can both agree that nothing about this situation is optimal. But what do you want to do about it? Because I wasn't hearing a lot of options from anyone."

Polly held her arms tightly around her body and crossed her legs so that she looked like she was turning herself into a pretzel. "If Serephine is a soul in the wrong body—and the body is one we're broadcasting into hell—why don't we just turn off the projector?"

Myles almost considered the idea, but the little girl deserved better. "She'd be nothing more than a soul with no direction and no grounding. Since there's no direct portal from hell to Guinee, Serephine would first have to go through all seven gates, from hell to life, on her own. That would turn her into a ghost in our world—another lost soul. Then, because she didn't simply die, she'd have to go through all seven gates, from life to Guinee, and without anyone to guide her. Once there, I'm sure the loas of the dead would take pity on her, but you're talking about fourteen gates that even a sane person would find daunting. If we made her body disappear, we'd be condemning her to a fate far worse than death."

Polly slightly eased up on her determined stance. "I just think Professor Yates might be able to help. His little diorama did aid in finding the vault."

From the way Kendell slammed the locks on the shutters, Myles knew she was about to argue that time was too precious to spend on another useless investigation. But the band needed something to do other than sit around the club, waiting for an update.

"You and the girls go see what you can find out while Kendell and I make our way into hell. Sanguine still needs to get Colin out to the swamp, so we've got a little time. We'll meet back here in an hour. Hopefully, Kendell and I will be on the other side of the conference call by then."

"We've got one more chore first." Kendell pointed at the cane in Myles's hand. "When we stuck that headpiece on the cane, we had Sanguine's energy and Baron Samedi's help, but we were the ones who did the real work. I'm sure we'll get along fine without them. Grab your instruments, girls. I'll meet you onstage."

The band marched into the club with all the enthusiasm of a group about to play a funeral dirge. Myles followed the procession by grabbing a metal chair from the courtyard and setting it in front of the stage. "Just one last time, and you'll never have to play another Dead or Alive song—at least not in reference to the musical group." A smattering of chuckles was the best he could get for the forced joke. As escort to the guest of honor, he took his seat, held the cane out in front of him, and turned the silver skull toward the band. He was no more enthusiastic about witnessing the performance than the group was about playing onstage. Any one-hit-wonder group that was popular before he was born reminded him too much of tending bar in the Quarter.

Every member of Polly Urethane and the Strippers faced the headpiece and sang "You Spin Me Round" while twirling their fingers in a counterclockwise direction. Like a drunk dude so infatuated with the group of women that he couldn't keep his head on straight, the silver skull followed the direction of the fingers until it spun off of the cane and fell to the floor.

With the silver headpiece removed, Myles put his hand on top of the glowing green crystal that had nestled underneath the hollow skull. The light illuminated his hand. The longer he held the top of the cane, the farther the glow radiated into his body. "I'm beginning to understand what Colin sees in this thing."

"Don't get carried away," Kendell said. "The minute we're back here, I'm sticking that locking skull back on the cane. Do you think you can make our plan work now?"

He aimed the cane at the front door of the club. "Now that the loas gifted me full use of the cane and you've freed it from the voodoo lock, walking between dimensions should be as easy as crossing the front threshold of the club. As for saving Serephine, that's going to take a little more work."

4

"*L*eave your cell phone on the bar." Sanguine expected to have her hands full with Colin in spite of his agreeing to Myles and Kendell's terms.

He slowly pulled it out of his coat and set it on the counter. "I could have my town car here in five minutes."

"We're not going to need it. I'll fly you out to the swamp."

She watched him for the inevitable disbelieving response. "Like hell you will."

"Being kept out of their way was your idea. If your car is close by, you might try something foolish. If I fly you out to my island, there's less likelihood you'll try to escape and interfere with their help."

He spread open his coat. "Do you want to frisk me as well? I might have some dangerous weapon you don't know about."

As opposed to the one I do know about? Nice cock reference, asshole. "As your only way back to the Quarter, I'll take my chances." She looked up through the opening between the buildings. "Face away from me, and fold your arms over your chest."

"You're serious about this? If we're going to fly, you could at least give me back my long coat. We could soar through the air side by side."

If she was going to get him all the way out to the swamp before Myles and Kendell walked through the door to hell, she was going to have to hustle. "We don't have time for your foolishness. I realize putting your life in the hands of a woman doesn't come naturally, but you're just going to have to sack up. You did approach me and the others about helping Serephine."

As Sanguine had hoped, using the name of Colin's daughter convinced him to do as directed. She lingered a minute to enjoy his embarrassment in standing with his back to her like a little boy about to be punished.

"Just be quick about it," he said.

"This will be a long flight. Try not to squirm. I wouldn't want to drop you into Lake Pontchartrain." She wrapped her arms around his stomach and lunged into the air.

Sanguine's relationship history included enough female companions for her to know when someone was feeling submissive in her arms, though she'd never before experienced the feeling of dominance over a man—especially one who prided himself on always being in control. The way Colin quivered under her command left her wondering if she'd dismissed the idea of being a dominatrix too soon.

She spread her wings to their full extent and beat them with all of her strength. Even with a ten-foot wingspan, the combined body weight of over three hundred pounds was a lot to keep airborne. The exertion had her panting by the time they'd made the open water of the lake.

"You sure you can make it out to the swamp? We can always turn back. There's no disgrace in admitting your limitations." His fear only helped fuel her determination.

"If you don't want me to fly off into the future and dump your ass in the lake at a time when no one will find you, you'd better shut up. In my irritation, I might not be able to work my way back to you when the time is right."

The threat worked. He remained quiet for the remainder of the trip across the lake.

By the time Sanguine spotted the spillway that separated the open water from the Mississippi River and the bayou beyond, her wings were shaking from exhaustion. She spread them out wide and banked toward the cypress grove in the distance. "Almost there."

His hands crept down from his elbows to caress her arms. The physical act of encouragement gave her the strength to hunch her shoulders and pour the last of her reserve energy into the aching back muscles that drove the tendons to her wings. When she saw the cabin hanging in the trees, she breathed a little easier. Though she'd done her best to stay focused, until that moment, she couldn't be sure she hadn't accidentally flown into the future or past. She spread her wings for one last glide down to the field in the middle of the island.

Once she let him go, Colin stretched out his back and

arms as if he'd been the one doing the work. "No food, no beverage service—there wasn't even a glass of water on that flight."

Much as she loved flying, it felt good to be back on the ground. "The flight crew was spread a little thin. My grandmother's old cabin is up in those trees."

He looked up and groaned. "I remember my first time on this island. You looked like a teenager when you greeted me with that shotgun aimed at my stomach. That seems like a lifetime ago."

"It was. You were still Lincoln Laroque back then, and I still had aspirations of returning to college." She didn't see much point in rehashing the past. If she were really interested in what might have been, she could easily fly through time to find out.

"I suppose that rotted-out house is the best we can do for shelter." He started toward the trail that led to the far side of the island.

I don't remember inviting you inside. She didn't press the issue. They had plenty of time to get into a fight later—no point in starting one the moment they'd landed. "I'm not even sure the water pump works. I haven't been out here in this time frame for quite a while."

"If we're back to a reality projection from the time around Hurricane Agnes, the pump doesn't work. I stayed out here for a night while chasing you through the swamp."

Nettles from the bushes that lined the unmaintained path were catching in her feathers. "You sucked at tracking, by the way. I had to light bonfires at night just to make sure you were following along and didn't get lost."

"You will remember who had the last laugh. My men were lying in wait when we finally emerged from your beloved swamp."

Whatever. She pushed ahead of him when they reached the tree with the nailed boards that led up to the cabin. "Better let me go up first. If I fall, at least I can spread my wings for a soft landing."

"You won't get an argument from me. Last time I was up there, I thought for sure the ghost of your dead grandmother was destroying her home just to make me fall out of her tree house."

Hopefully, that was the case. If not, these boards might really be paper-thin from rot. She held her wings at the ready as she trusted her weight to the first improvised step. Memories of scampering up the rungs while her grandmother yelled for her to be careful made Sanguine feel old. When the tops of her wings hit the trapdoor, she reached overhead and pushed open the access to the porch. "I seem to have made it."

"Suddenly, I'm less concerned about wounding my male pride in having you fly me in your arms." He bounced on the first step as if trying to prove the ladder unstable.

She peered down from the trap door. "Would you prefer me to come down and hold your hand?" She couldn't resist the snarky teasing.

"No, but if I break a bone, I expect you to fetch my town car."

Sanguine looked around the dusty rooms she'd grown up in for some indication of how long her grandmother had been gone. Each time she'd flown out to the swamp in hell, she'd seen her grandmother's home perched in the field, but then, she'd also encountered the old woman while she was still in her prime. *I miss you, Grandma, but maybe it's better you don't see me with the devil you spent your life trying to contain.*

Colin stood on the porch and brushed the stickers off his slacks. "So how shall we spend our time? Did the old woman leave a deck of cards or something?"

"Why? You want me to read your future?" Sanguine felt a little defensive about where she'd grown up.

"I don't doubt it would be full of terrors." He poked his head into her grandmother's room. "Just the one bedroom? Where did you sleep?"

"In a hammock on the porch during the summer. When it got cold or rainy, I slept on the couch. I've never been one for needing a specific space to call my own."

He pulled off his wrinkled coat. "I'm afraid that flight did a number on my suit."

Nice try, buddy. "I'm not having sex with you, if that's what you're implying."

He looked around the cabin as if searching for a suitable spot. "I wouldn't dream of it."

Right. Like you're too high-class to put your bare ass on any piece of furniture in my home? I know full well you got it on with random women in the disgusting alley beside the club. She sat in one of the two kitchen chairs so she could spread her wings while letting her irritation subside. "Why is saving Serephine so important to you? I could understand using her as one of your experiments to steal souls from Guinee, but trying to heal her goes beyond your normally calculated endeavors."

He sat on the edge of the couch cushion as if trying not to further soil his suit. "I'm not trying to *steal* anyone. But you're just going to have to stay in my hell for me to prove I mean what I say. As for Serephine, you wouldn't believe me, so what's the point in discussing it?"

"We have all day. I don't know what Myles and Kendell can do for your little girl, but I can't imagine it'll be simply a snap of the fingers."

He shrugged as if his answer didn't really matter. "I loved her."

Bullshit. "That's an awfully simple answer."

She saw something new in his eyes that seemed almost human. "The day she died was the day I gave up on caring about people. My family life at the time was no prize—though I had no one to blame but myself. Fleurentine hated me for my womanizing. I tried to keep my business practices—and the brothels that were stocked from those activities—secret from her, but I always suspected she knew about the indentured prostitutes. Since I was constantly either at work or parties, Antoine took over the job of protecting Serephine. But when I was home, that little girl lit up so brightly she could turn the darkest night into day—all because of me. I'd never known that kind of love, and I haven't experienced it since. The longer I exist, the more precious I realize it was, and I threw it away."

"So your concern for her really is all about you again. You don't really love her. You just miss having her adoration."

He looked at his scuffed-up shoes. "I knew you wouldn't understand. She saw something in me that no one ever had. I could see the good man I might have been reflected in her eyes. While condemned to your hell, I met an alternate version of Serephine as a grown-up. She hated me, but she also told me that the man she'd seen as a little girl was possible. I took the wrong path, and the daughter I knew suffered for it."

"So you see bringing her back to life as penance for all of your evil?"

He motioned to the room. "You condemned me to this realm because you thought my selfishness and greed were best isolated from the human continuum. I see Serephine as the opposite of what you see in me. Her optimism and love would have elevated everyone she met. The world became a darker place when she left it. Returning her to the reservoir of our collective spirit like the loas of the dead intend would only dilute her spark until it had no meaning. Some people deserve to have their day in the sun. And no one lit up this world more than Serephine. Condemn me if you wish, but if opposites attract, might it also be true that a devilish person could give rise to an angel?"

Sanguine knew he was talking about his daughter, but her wings quivered as if he were talking about her. "Are you sure you're not just hoping to redeem your reputation by giving the world your daughter?"

"She never knew the man I became. And after messing up her soul by trying to pull her out of Guinee, I doubt any future story she would tell about me would be favorable. If I were to look for someone to tell my side of things, you're the one I'd turn to—not a seven-year-old girl who knew so little of life."

"I'm not playing the game of arguing your merits." The late-afternoon light as the sun shone through cypress branches began turning the room into a ghostly display of moving shadows. "If she was the ultimate prize you tried to snag from Guinee, why didn't you wait until you knew what you were doing or ask for help? For a soul you held as being so precious, you sure messed things up."

"I did ask for your help, but I couldn't wait forever for your reply. I knew I might only get one chance, and time was running out. Expecting Myles to give me the cane and the loas of the dead to be subdued enough to let me set up shop again in their domain were calculated risks. I still believe my idea for saving human souls from death was a good plan, but in the case of Serephine's resurrection, I couldn't rely on so many variables when I had an alternate means of pulling her across right at my fingertips. And even if you did deny me your help, I knew if things went wrong, you'd have my back."

"WHERE DO WE EVEN START?" Kendell had expected the child to be in a bad way, but nothing had prepared her for the drooling, wild-eyed, self-destructive animal-child that hurled herself at the walls and babbled incoherently. She reminded Kendell of a horror story character confined to an insane asylum.

Myles kept his arm around Kendell's waist as if

protecting her, though she wasn't sure if it was from the child or from the impulse to dive in to help. "We know that she has three problems: her sense of time is out of whack, she's in the wrong body, and she's been pulled out of her dimension. Until she calms down, I don't see how we can address any of those issues. You're the closest to having an inkling of what she's going through. Any thoughts?"

"Music worked to calm me down, but only because it's so personal to me. The band gave me a reference to focus on —kind of like a drowning person seeing a lighthouse on the shore. But it still took all my willpower to make the swim."

From behind them came a gentle lullaby. The words were so soft and quiet she doubted the child, in her fit of rage, would know that anyone was singing. The motherly expression of love, however, wasn't as much about volume as pure emotion. She turned to Miss Fleur and whispered, "Stand close so she can see you."

By the third repeat of "All Through the Night," Kendell had the music memorized. Someone needed to get down to the child, who sat against the wall with her arms wrapped around her legs, rocking to her mother's voice. Though still a slobbering mess, at least Serephine had stopped trying to destroy her body in an attempt to free her soul.

Kendell pointed toward the pit, indicating she was going to join the girl. Myles didn't object, but he looked concerned. She'd have liked to reassure him that she knew what she was doing, but she feared any sound other than Miss Fleur's singing would break the motherly spell. A kiss on Myles's cheek was the best she could do to ease his anxiety.

The stone steps were slippery under her tennis shoes, but the combination of rubber and rock didn't make any unwanted sound. When she reached the bottom, she hunched down against the wall, mirroring the position of the girl across the room. *First, we need to stabilize your concept of time. Miss Fleur would only be fifty years ahead of you when she died here in this convent. It's a start, but I need to bring you the remaining hundred years into my time.*

Kendell started humming along with the soft voice above. Serephine's body tightened up so badly Kendell feared the girl was having a seizure. She wanted to rush to the child and hold her tightly as an act of support, but for Serephine to cross time and dimension, she would need to do her part. *I can't make the first move. That would only give you an excuse to dive deeper into yourself. You have to try and find your way out of your personal hell, Serephine.*

The girl turned her crystal-blue eyes to Kendell. Her look of terror and despair was tempered with a growing understanding of what was happening. *Good girl. Just focus on the singing and me.*

At the end of an hour, Serephine had fallen asleep. Kendell carefully got to her feet and motioned for Myles and Miss Fleur to come down. She and Fleurentine had succeeded in calming the girl, but saving her soul wouldn't be so simple.

Even after the other two joined her, Kendell couldn't brave crossing the room. Serephine's sleep was far from restful. Her body jerked as if she were fighting a horde of demons.

"What are we supposed to do now?" Kendell feared they were badly out of their depth.

Myles worked his hand over the top of the cane. "Since this convent is an interdimensional embassy, she's still not fixed in a specific time. At least she seems to have accepted whatever reality she's experiencing. That's a start. I can take her soul through dimensions the way you and I played cat and mouse with Colin. Without the conflict of being in her body, Serephine might gain a fresh understanding of who she is. Hopefully, once she no longer sees all of us as demons, we'll be able to reason with her. Explaining how this strange body is now hers is going to take some doing, though."

With every word he whispered, Kendell worried the frightened girl would wake up. "One problem at a time. Can you make the journey while she's asleep?"

He looked from Kendell to Miss Fleur. "Even with both of us as just spirits, I can't risk her waking up between dimensions. I'll need one of you to come with me to keep her calm."

Miss Fleur pulled her shawl around her shoulders. "Just tell me what to do."

Kendell accepted that Serephine's mother would be the best choice, but she couldn't just stand around, waiting for the trio to return. "Keep singing that lullaby. We'll start off together so Serephine can feel the harmony we're creating between our times. I'll keep singing from this dimension while Myles takes you on a little joyride. Our voices will move out of sync, but that distortion will provide a musical roadmap for Serephine, like breadcrumbs left on a trail.

Between our two voices, hopefully we'll not just cross her over dimensions, but we'll also heal her time imbalance."

～

MYLES CARESSED Kendell's back as she harmonized with Miss Fleur. Serephine was still sleeping but barely. He needed to hold the girl in his arms, though he was more than a little concerned about how she would react to being touched by some strange dude after fighting off demons. Hopefully, having her mother next to her would help. He aimed his cane at Serephine, indicating to Miss Fleur that it was time.

While sleeping, Serephine's body had convulsed, moving from sitting in a ball to stretched out straight. She'd finally ended up curled on the floor in a fetal position. Myles lay on the cold stone floor to cuddle the emotionally battered girl with one arm while holding the cane tightly to his chest with the other. Miss Fleur lay in front of her daughter and stroked the girl's hair and shoulders while continuing to sing the lullaby.

The position wasn't optimal for interdimensional travel, but keeping the girl calm was Myles's top priority. If either Miss Fleur or Serephine broke out of his psychic bond while traveling between dimensions, she'd be swept into chaos like someone falling out of a lifeboat in stormy seas. He closed his eyes and circled his hand up to the walking stick's green crystal. *Here we go.*

Miss Fleur's soft singing remained the same, but Kendell's voice faded and intensified as if someone were trying to tune in to a song on an old-fashioned radio. He used her voice as a reference point while spinning through the dimensions that surrounded Serephine. In each realm, the girl remained a terrified creature unable to connect to reality. *We need to go deeper. I need to find that child who saved us from the Laurette mansion while it was burning.*

He focused on his own time line and traced back to the confrontation with Colin. Using the cane like a joystick, he moved into the dimension that Colin had visited before the fire. When he spotted the Laurette mansion in all of its historic elegance, he pulled up on the staff to stop the swirling images. Myles stood beside Miss Fleur in the entryway with Serephine in his arms, the three of them getting their bearings like stranded travelers just in from the cold.

A woman sat on a divan in the foyer of the elegant Garden District home. From her stylish blue skirt, jacket, and white silk blouse, Myles could tell they'd landed in what he knew to be the present in his time line. Serephine remained sleeping.

Myles leaned in to Miss Fleur so as not to wake the child. "I'm not sure where we ended up."

The strange woman stood and smoothed her dress. She walked up to them as if they were guests she'd been expecting for some time. She pointed at the child. "Is this her?"

Miss Fleur stepped forward and took the woman's hands, staring so hard into her eyes that Myles wondered if he was going to have another person to save. "It's you, isn't it?"

The woman turned back toward Serephine. "Yes. That's me in Myles's arms. Or at least an alternate-reality version of me. From the time our father nearly beat down my door in that hell of his, I knew this poor child would find me one day." She turned back to Miss Fleur. "What has that idiot done now, Mother?"

It didn't take long for Miss Fleur to explain the situation, though Myles thought the woman overly romanticized Colin's desire to save his daughter. In the journey of pure spiritual energy, the young child no longer looked like the body she'd been cast into by Colin. She'd reverted to the image she still held of herself as the girl who'd died so long ago. The straight strawberry-blond hair of her replacement body had become curls and ringlets of shimmering white.

The adult version of Sere had let her hair grow long enough that the unruly locks had become gentle waves. "What can I do to help?"

How am I supposed to know? I'm not a doctor of the soul—just the ambulance driver. "She needs to remember who she truly is. All we can do is tell her who she is to us. None of us can see deep enough into her soul or understand how that connects to who she may become."

The woman smoothed the girl's disheveled hair from her eyes. "It's okay, Sere. I know you're not sleeping. Open your eyes." The woman's tone was unnecessarily brusque.

The girl opened her eyes and struggled down from Myles's arms. "What do you want with me?"

Serephine the adult didn't even bother bending down to the girl's level. Her stance wasn't one of domineering authority, but her straight-ahead face with down-turned eyes carried the message *Grow up* loud and clear. "I'm here to tell you to stop acting like a little girl. You and I both know who you really are. Your mother and father thought they were raising a sweet, demure little angel. They never bothered to see how much strength it took to take your own life."

The child cocked her head with a similar look of command. "You weren't that brave?"

"My bravery took me on a different path than yours did. But then, the man we both called father took two different paths as well. I only know the man you grew up with by looking down at your history. I'm here to tell you one thing and one thing only: you are a badass. Start acting like it."

Miss Fleur's breathing was so intense that Myles could hear it. "She's right, Sere. Your father wanted an innocent version of me, but what neither of us saw was the strength you got from him—not his evil desires but his force of will. If you're going to survive this world, you'll need more than I was able to give you."

Serephine the adult turned to the ghost of her mother. "The woman I see before me also had multiple time lines. You've got more strength than you know. As this child grows, hopefully she'll have a chance to discover the real you."

Myles had met enough seers to know when one was standing in front of him. "Will Sere grow up to see alternate dimensions as well?"

Serephine turned back to the child. "It's hard to say. She's already been through enough to detect the changes, but in the artificial body she inhabits back in the abbey, who she grows up to be is anyone's guess."

"But you said I was a badass," Sere said. "If you can't see my future, how do you know?"

"You're the daughter of the devil being raised by an angel. It doesn't take any special abilities to see what's possible for you. But with such powerful people in your life, you're going to have to step up in order to control your own destiny. I still remember what it was like to be your age— who I was and who you still are. You can stop pretending you fit into other people's plans for you."

"How do I do that?" the girl asked.

"Be bold. Be aggressive. Don't worry about being wrong if what you're fighting for is something you believe in. Accept the strengths your father put in you, but be cautious of his failings. There will always be people around to guide you. Choose your mentors with care."

Young Sere's trusting blue eyes made Myles want to protect her from the life the older woman must have seen, but the girl sounded almost relieved at being told she could do more than what was expected of her. "Will I ever see you again?"

"Maybe. Your life is so different from mine that I'm only able to see into your near future. If you follow my advice, you'll surpass anything I could imagine."

Sere walked over to Myles and took his hand. "It's time we went home."

"Are you sure you don't want to meet other versions of yourself? We can travel to as many dimensions as you need."

The child shook her head. "If I'm going to be a badass, it's time I got started."

~

Though Kendell enjoyed the lullaby, after the hundredth rendition, her voice was beginning to falter. Without accompaniment, keeping to the rhythm established by Miss Fleur was a bit like banging her head against a wall, but she dared not miss a beat. Myles was relying on her to navigate the way home.

When she finally saw them moving on the floor as though coming out of a deep sleep, she gave up on continuing the song. Seeing Serephine sit up between Myles and Miss Fleur almost distracted Kendell from hugging Myles, but she knelt on the floor and wrapped her arms around him so hard she thought she might bruise him. "How did it go?"

He remained on the floor as he came back to full consciousness. "Unexpectedly. We traveled into an alternate time line for Sere. She got to meet an adult version of herself."

"She was nice."

Sere's words made Kendell look down into the light-blue eyes. "Are you feeling better? You look better."

The girl leaned back in her mother's arms. "I still don't know what's happened to me. This body feels like a dress that doesn't fit. It itches." She looked around the room made of stone and lined with old mattresses. "But the demons have left this place."

Kendell desperately wanted to caress the child's strawberry-blond hair, but Sere's quizzical eyes made it clear she was still processing her surroundings. Kendell remembered the feeling of coming out of the demon realm and how paper-thin the divide between dimensions had appeared. Serephine could all too easily revert back to the nightmare she'd just escaped.

"You have experienced something that not many people are able to endure," Kendell said.

Instead of looking concerned, as Kendell had expected, the little girl smiled as if she had just been paid a compliment. "I'm stronger than most people."

Myles reached out and caressed the girl's straight hair. "Yes, you are. Now that you've joined our time through Kendell and your mother's singing, and found your way back to who you are by meeting a version of yourself, do you feel up to working on that body? It will involve going outside. We'll have to leave the convent. That might be pretty scary. If you start feeling like you're falling back into that nightmare, just tell us. Kendell will keep singing to you. That seemed to help. If it gets too bad, we can come back here."

Sere looked at her mother. "Are you coming too?"

Miss Fleur put her hand on the girl's slender shoulders. "I can't leave the convent. You can trust these two. They came here to help you."

The girl looked back at Kendell. "Are you two superheroes?"

"How do you know that term?" Kendell wasn't sure she wanted to hear the answer.

"I don't know. It's just in my head. There's a lot of stuff in there that I don't understand." She looked at Kendell with more curiosity than fear. "How did it get in there?"

Myles leaned on his cane to get off the floor. "Your body and soul are misaligned. I suspect that whatever you're receiving from the projection in life isn't just flesh and bone. The sooner we get you comfortable in that body, the better."

Sere turned back to Kendell. "You didn't answer my question."

Kendell wondered if this was how her parents felt when she wouldn't let go of something. "We're not superheroes. At least, I don't think we are."

Sere scrunched up her face as if she were working out an idea. "You are to me."

Miss Fleur put her hand against the wall in an attempt to stand, but she only made it halfway before slumping back to the floor. "I think someone needs to help me back to my room. That trip seems to have taken it out of me."

"What is it, Mama?" Sere asked.

One look at the woman's ghostly-white complexion told Kendell the ailment was more than exhaustion. "Myles can stay with you, Sere. I'll help your mother back to the nuns."

"Thank you, my dear." The woman's forced smile looked to be hiding a soul in tatters.

Kendell wrapped her arm around the woman's waist and helped her to her feet. With each step, Miss Fleur trusted more of her weight to Kendell's shoulders. "I'll have you back to your bed in no time."

"Just get me out of sight of Sere," Miss Fleur whispered. "She can't see me die."

As she moved the woman from the room, Kendell tried to make it look like she was taking her time, but Miss Fleur's words sent panic through her steps. "You'll be fine once we get you settled."

"You and I know that's not true. The nuns warned me about taking too many meetings through their embassy. I suspect they aren't going to be very happy with me for having left this spiritual plane, but sacrificing what's left of my life was worth it to save Sere."

Though the woman wasn't heavy, each step up the stone staircase required careful footing to prevent her falling.

"Are you in pain?"

"No, but my grasp on reality is slipping. Promise me you'll take care of Sere. Don't leave her in this hell alone with Colin."

Kendell wondered how one little girl could inspire such passion. "She will always be surrounded by love. You can rest easy. We will be her family."

At the top of the stairs, Brother Aramis and the Reverend Mother took Miss Fleur in their arms. The old nun cast an accusing glare at Kendell. "We've got her. Take care of that child before she suffers the same fate. A soul can only exist for a short time when it's out of sync with its surroundings."

Kendell rushed down the stairs with a renewed urgency. Though they'd solved two out of Sere's three spiritual problems, she couldn't image how they were going to finish transplanting the girl's soul into the new body. She took a deep breath at the bottom of the stairs. "It's time we checked in with the band. Professor Yates will want to know what we're dealing with. Hopefully, by now he's figured out how to stabilize body and soul."

Myles gave her a half nod of understanding then turned to the girl. "Do you trust me?"

The girl looked up at Myles, gripping his hand. "Just don't leave me."

Kendell's heart ached to hear those words.

"Never," Myles said. "Keep hold of my hand. If you feel weak, I'll carry you. Once we get to the club and talk to our friends, we'll figure out a way to make you feel much better."

Sere took Kendell's hand as well. "Will Mother be okay?"

Kendell found it hard to talk past the lump in her throat. "I hope so."

Getting through the convent dormitory without exposing Sere to the rush of people attending Miss Fleur was a challenge, but the nuns walked with their customary calm determination without displaying any panic on seeing the child. Kendell wanted to offer some words of encouragement to the caregivers, but the trusting hand in hers made it impossible to speak without breaking down.

Myles led the way out of the building and into the sun-drenched yard. "Your alternate self was right. You're a very brave girl, Sere."

"I don't feel well."

Myles scooped her up and put her on his shoulders. "Just hang on. We'll be with friends soon."

Kendell started singing the lullaby before they left the

front gate. Her fear for the child made it hard to control her voice.

Myles held onto the girl's legs. "Have you ever ridden a horse?"

Her eyes were drooping, and she seemed to be having trouble keeping her balance. "A long time ago."

"Well, hang on, and I'll do my best horse trot for you." He broke into a steady jog.

Running made it even harder to sing, but each time Kendell stopped, Sere started jerking as if she were having a seizure. Her mumbling was accompanied by wild shakes of her head. As they turned the corner toward the club, Kendell was grateful they'd made it that far without the girl slipping into a coma or, worse, an alternate reality.

Myles swung Sere off his shoulders and into his embrace before opening the door. His worried look conveyed to Kendell what he didn't want to say.

She nodded. Their only hope was that Professor Yates had figured out the problem and had a solution at the ready. Sere's connection to the strange body wasn't going to last long at that rate. The music had kept her calm, but like a sedative, it was only masking the problem. Kendell ran ahead and had the speakeasy open before Myles carried Sere into the courtyard.

In the land of the living, the band was already seated with Professor Yates when Myles finished drawing the veve that activated the gate. He took Sere onto his lap. "Her body and soul aren't matched up. That's about all I know."

Like a physician diagnosing a mental illness, Professor

Yates stared at the child. "Is she talking like someone from the 1800s, or is she at ease with modern life?"

"She's not at ease with anything," Kendell said.

Myles put his hand on Kendell's back. "She called us superheroes. When we asked how she knew the term, she'd didn't have an answer. Her use of language doesn't sound odd, so I'd guess she's more at home with modern day than when she was a girl in the 1800s. Other than that, she knows she's Serephine Malveaux, and she recognized her mother. Now that she's away from her father, she's been going by Sere. I'm not sure if that's an emotional-comfort thing or a desire to modernize her name."

Professor Yates nodded. "I expected something like that. Any fundamental understanding of life that she learned in the 1800s has become a part of who she is—like emotional scars or feelings of love. She has retained that level of self-awareness from her previous life. But traditional learning, like math or science, she acquired from the brain of the child we're projecting. She's basically trying to reconcile two streams of mental awareness."

Polly stood beside the professor. "What can we do? Clearly, she doesn't have time for philosophical ramblings."

He shook his head as if realizing he'd let his speculations get the better of him. "We need to modify that body into accepting a soul. If Sere is still with us, as she clearly is, then the problem isn't with her spirit. Children are much more pliable in accepting a changing reality than adults."

Polly put her hand on the man's shoulder. "How do we modify her projection?"

"Ultimately, she needs to be self-sufficient. We can't let

her be dependent on the power we're sending into hell forever. But for her immediate needs, we'll need to increase the energy sent to her body. That's going to drain what we provide to the rest of our virtual reality."

"At this point, it no longer matters," Kendell said. "Colin knows what we did. That's old news. Use all the energy you need. Just save her."

"You do realize this is paranormally derived energy," the haggard man said. "It's not like we're just using a stronger battery to make a toy run longer. The marionette people in that hell of yours were meant to entertain Colin, not support a human soul. If we're successful in making her new body independent of our support, I don't know what that magic will do to her."

Myles held Sere to his chest. "As always, let's just face one problem at a time. Colin wants his child revived, but the loas of the dead have other ideas for Sere's soul. At this point, I don't intend on giving her to either authority. Once she's made whole, those two entities are going to be our next concern. Sere needs to be her own person. She has that right. What magic she might possess from our cure will have to wait until later."

Professor Yates pulled out his cell phone and turned to Polly. "Let's get started. I've developed an app to remotely control the equipment. You watch the girl through the gate while I dial up more power. I don't want to overdo it, but we need to get that child back on her feet."

Polly signaled to the rest of the band, and all four women hunkered down in front of the gate. "We're going to sing to you, Sere. When you feel up to it, we want you to sing along if you can, okay?"

Kendell hoped the nod from the groggy girl in Myles's arms was an acknowledgement and not just a sign that she was fading away.

Polly started quietly singing "Come as You Are." By the second time through, Minerva had added a soft rhythm by tapping on the metal table. Even without their instruments, the band was able to ramp up the energy of their singing in time with the power Professor Yates was sending to the child's body.

Sere popped off of Myles's lap, stood in front of the band, and started bellowing out the words with wild abandon. Her shouting echoed off the brick walls. At first, Kendell was relieved to hear the child reveling in her body's newfound power, but when the fog bank lowered over the club, she started to fear that too much energy had been sapped from life's projection.

The band members lowered their voices, indicating that Professor Yates was dialing back his instruments. Sere continued to sing at full volume, but her decibel level fell back to a normal human range.

Polly was out of breath from singing. "And I thought my brother's kids were loud."

---

5

*K*endell held Sere's hand as the two of them walked out of the club. Myles, the band, and Professor Yates could discuss the long-term plan for stabilizing the child without her having to listen in. A dense fog remained over the city. Kendell couldn't see farther than a block in any direction. "How do you feel?"

"Like my brain is channel surfing. I can't focus on anything for more than a few seconds."

You guys better figure out something better than this damn fog. "Let's go walk by the river. I find the water helps calm my thoughts."

The girl scuffed her shoes on the concrete sidewalk, slowing the pace even more. She kept her head down. "Are you going to take care of me now?"

The simple sweetness of the question made Kendell want to cry. "I wish I could, but Myles and I will have to return to our lives. This isn't our dimension."

"I guess superheroes don't make good parents."

She squeezed the girl's small hand. "I have a friend who won't leave you, though. She's an honest-to-God angel."

Sere looked up with excitement in her eyes. "The kind with wings?"

"Her wings are ten feet wide. She even flew me across the river once."

"Where is she now?" Sere asked.

Kendell couldn't bring herself to explain the complex relationship between Sanguine and the girl's father. "She's taking care of another problem, but she'll be here soon."

"Is she another superhero like you?" Serephine stopped dragging her feet and started skipping alongside Kendell.

"I guess you could say that. I think of her as a heroine. I suppose *super* isn't a bad addition. Would you like an angel looking out for you?"

Sere resumed her normal walk while considering the question. "I want someone who will teach me to be a badass. That's what the other me said I was supposed to be."

I wonder if teaching a child swear words is bad if the person teaching is actually herself. "So you'd like to stay in that body?"

Again, Sere gave the question the time it took to pass a few buildings before she had an answer. "I don't want to go back to Guinee. I wasn't there for very long, but I didn't like it."

Kendell could see how the realm filled with brothels, bars, and casinos wouldn't be fitting for a small child. "Weren't the loas of the dead nice to you?"

"Maman Brigitte looked after me. She was nice, but her husband, Baron Samedi, didn't like me very much."

Kendell wondered how much of the loa's reserve toward the child had more to do with her father, Baron Malveaux, and his future usurping of the loa's power over the seventh gate—not to mention the theft of his cane. "He had some issues with your father."

"Everyone has issues with Papa. I guess he's not a very nice man."

Another topic I can't discuss with you. "He's trying to be better." Kendell looked down at the child who'd already been through so much. "I don't think any of us has asked what you want. I mean, not just who to look after you but what realm you'd like to live in as well."

"I don't like Guinee, and I don't know anyone in your world anymore—except you and Myles. If you can't take care of me, I'll be lost in your world." She looked into the fog. "I just want someone to love me. Is that possible?"

I wish you were here, Sanguine. "I'll make sure of it."

WITH AN INTERIM PLAN IN PLACE, Myles switched his gate connection from talking to the band and Professor Yates to accepting the request from Sanguine's gate out in the swamp. Being in the same dimension was a bit like talking over the phone to someone in the same house—no dialing necessary.

Colin's face dominated the connection. "How is she?"

Myles decided to let the man squirm for a while until his

true motivation became clear. "She was in a bad way. We nearly lost her a couple of times. Even now, I doubt she's the same little girl you remember. She's grown up a lot in just a few hours."

"But she's alive? The loas of the dead didn't take her?"

That's really all you care about? "This isn't a game. I didn't make the trip out here just so you could rub your success in the loas' faces. Now that she's whole again, Papa Ghede is going to demand the return of her soul."

"You can't do that. Let me see her." Colin's desperation seemed genuine, but then, most of what he did seemed sincere at some point.

"Kendell took her for a walk to help acclimate her to this realm and her new body."

Colin finally backed up enough to address Sanguine. "We have time. You could fly me back to the Quarter. I can't let him take her back to Guinee. At least let me make my plea in person."

Sanguine's wings were half-spread and her arms crossed. "You're not in a position to request anything. All we agreed to was helping Serephine. Your part of the arrangement is to stay as far away as possible."

He raised his hand to her. "Only while she was being saved. If she's better now, I can return to see her. I never agreed to not seeing her. We can wait until Myles and Kendell return to life, but I don't want to leave Serephine alone for very long. She is just a child."

Myles had known the fight was coming from the moment they'd agreed to postpone the decision of what to do with Sere once she was whole. He had his arguments ready. "I'm not leaving her here for you like a bag of groceries in the trunk of a car waiting to be brought inside. You might have been her father at one time, but you lost that privilege when she took her life."

"I rescued her from Guinee." Now that he'd gotten what he wanted, Colin's defiance was in stark contrast to his initial request for help.

"I'm not having you back here in the Quarter, where you can try again to steal my cane. As for Serephine, she's no longer your responsibility."

From the way Colin scrunched up his face then slowly released the tension, his attempt at emotional control was clearly causing him physical pain. "All I'm asking is for you and I to meet over drinks to discuss our issues. I've never been a fan of talking over connections—be they powered by electricity or magic. You can hide your cane in Delphine's shop if it makes you feel better."

I'd rather have it with me so I can rap you over the head with it and send you into another dimension. Instead of continuing the argument, Myles turned to Sanguine. "We do need you back here. There are some things to discuss."

"You're not leaving me out here in the swamp alone." Colin sounded panicked, like a little kid who was afraid of being left alone in the dark.

Sanguine looked at Myles through the connection. "He has a point. My alligators have been eyeing him all day from the marsh grasses. We're not going to solve anything with him out here anyway. Now that you've taken care of the most pressing crises, we can negotiate the peace. Colin is aware of the fact that he's indebted to you."

Myles strongly doubted her gators would do anything without her permission, but keeping Colin on his toes while out in the swamp had to be a full-time job. "I'm holding you responsible if he starts playing his devilish games again."

"We'll fly to Spanish Plaza. You can meet us there. That way, we can all see Serephine together."

～

KENDELL LOVED the view of the river, even if it was shrouded in fog. Some moments she wished could last forever. With Sere sitting next to her, she imagined herself as the girl's mother. Myles had been so caring and sweet toward the child. Never before had Kendell thought of him as father material, but he still had his ways of surprising her. "I can see why Colin wanted you back. I just wish he were the kind of father you deserve."

Sere swung her feet back and forth under the metal bench. "He's better than you think."

"Maybe so. Your mother seemed to think he still had redeeming qualities. He needs to control those devilish desires, though. It's always one step forward then one leap backward with him."

Sere watched her shoes as if the feet doing the kicking were not her own. "So you think he's getting worse?"

Kendell had to replay her comment to figure out what the child meant. "I'm not sure. He gives me hope that he's changed, then he makes some bonehead move that proves he hasn't. Stealing your soul from Guinee and putting you in a strange body certainly wasn't his best idea."

"I could have said no. He didn't force me. Besides, you were the one who showed me I didn't have to stay with the loas."

Finding the girl in the old mansion then making her one of the guardians over her father's hell might not have been the smartest play either. "I guess we all do things we regret."

Sere put her hands in her lap. "You don't want me here?"

Kendell put her arm around the girl's small shoulders and pulled her close. "Of course I want you here. But you had to endure more than you should have, and that was partly my fault."

At first Kendell thought the disturbance in the fog was the effect of a passing ship. When she saw the giant white angel wings emerge from the gray clouds, however, she knew Sanguine was returning from the swamp.

Sere pointed at the angel. "She's so beautiful."

Kendell kept her arm around the girl. "That's the friend I was telling you about."

Sanguine dropped Colin at the far side of the walkway before settling to the ground in front of the bench. "Sorry to make such a dramatic entrance. What's with the fog bank? I thought Professor Yates's projection was stable."

"Sere needed more energy to keep her replacement body stable. Until we come up with a better solution, hell is going to be a little less populated."

The green glow opposite where Sanguine had landed indicated that Myles wasn't far away. Kendell got off the bench to prevent any possible confrontation with Colin. She yelled loud enough that both men would hear her. "Please keep this meeting civil for the child's sake."

Myles aimed the foot of the cane at Colin. "I'll play nice if he does."

This is not going to end well.

Sere petted Sanguine's wings as if the tension between the two men didn't matter. "They're so soft. What's it like to fly?"

The connection between the young girl and her guardian angel was palpable. Sanguine's wings stirred gently, and Kendell had a pretty good idea of what she was thinking of doing. With a nod, Kendell silently agreed to her friend's idea.

Sanguine knelt in front of the girl. "Would you like to go for a ride?"

As if afraid that anything she might say would break the spell, Sere nodded enthusiastically.

Colin took a few steps toward the gathering but stopped well short of the tip of Myles's cane. "I want to see my child first."

Sanguine lifted Sere into her arms and addressed Colin. "You've been given enough privileges. This sweet child doesn't need to be subjected to this discussion about her future." She ran toward the fog and took flight into the gray nothingness.

Once the angel and her ward were gone, the fog lifted. Instead of the waterfront teeming with tourists, however, there was only the empty hell that had existed before the professor's projections had gone into effect.

Colin turned around, surveying the area as if experiencing his hell for the first time. "What just happened?"

Kendell tried to stay between Myles and Colin to prevent a fight. "This is the price of keeping Serephine alive."

"I don't understand," Colin said. "The power from the World Trade Center should be more than enough to keep everything running as it was."

"Well, I guess you don't know everything, now, do you?" Myles remained standing, much to Kendell's relief.

She put her hand on his chest to remind him of the love that would hopefully keep him from striking out. "This is the hell Colin is bestowing on his daughter. Let him take it all in before you distract him with your anger."

"How far back does this realm go?" Colin asked. "Will time continue to move forward, or will it degenerate back to the posthurricane nightmare Agnes tossed me into?"

Myles finally set the foot of the cane on the ground. "Our team is working on a more permanent solution for Serephine, but for now, this is the best they've come up with. Drawing this much energy from the projection, however, will eventually reduce the fog into the world you're seeing."

"So she's not stable?" Colin asked.

Kendell had seen enough emotion from Colin to know that the fear in his eyes was genuine. With Myles no longer intent on bashing the man's brains in, she was able to redirect her attention to the distraught father. "We're not experts in what it takes to keep a person alive. You were the one who created this problem. Do *you* have any ideas?"

Colin stared into the fog as if seeking an answer in the gray mist. "While I ran the seventh gate to Guinee, there was a belief among the loas that a balance was needed between the living and the dead. That had to do with life and death, though, not hell. If this realm works under the same rules, a death in hell will be needed to sustain the new life. That's the only explanation I can come up with as to why Serephine would need so much energy."

Though she was partially responsible for hell, Kendell barely understood how it worked. "A death wasn't needed for you."

"Agnes Delarosa, Marie Laveau, and the loas of the dead all believed that my soul shouldn't be returned to the *deep waters*, so there was a mutual agreement to leave me here on permanent loan. Even so, this realm requires the energy of you and Sanguine to keep it running. That creates a balance between life and hell, if not death."

"So that's what Delphine meant when she said we were two sides of the cage," Kendell said.

Myles rotated the cane under his palm. "Could we find two more people to power up Serephine?"

"It doesn't work that way," Colin said. "The loas are very possessive of human energy. They'd never agree to a second permanent loan of a soul, especially not one they value."

Myles sat on the bench. "Then we're back to Papa Ghede's demand that Serephine return to Guinee."

Kendell had to move quickly to keep Colin from attacking Myles.

"You can't," Colin said as he tried to evade Kendell and get at Myles. "Send me instead, but don't sacrifice my sweet daughter."

Kendell doubted Colin was serious, but the idea was

worth pursuing. "If the loas don't want you, what would be the point?"

He backed up a pace. "They don't register every person who's born or dies. The way they keep an eye on the *deep waters* would be closer to a measuring stick to see how much water is in the reservoir—a very precise measuring stick."

"But they specifically don't want you," Myles said. "Even if you did agree to accepting the end of your existence in exchange for Serephine, you'd never make it through Guinee."

"They'll be expecting a soul that's been ripped to shreds. You saw Serephine when she was in the convent. Could you really tell who that person truly was?"

Kendell wanted to sit next to Myles, but she wasn't yet ready to trust that the two men wouldn't break into a fight, so she remained standing like a wall between them. "What are you proposing?"

"I can't enter Guinee without first returning to life," Colin said. "That means going through your magical seven gates. But once I'm among the living, Myles can go to Guinee and yank me through Guinee's seventh gate with his cane. The direct transfer should tear my soul similarly to what you saw in Serephine."

"Or what I experienced when you pulled me into hell." Kendell's memories of the event would never fade even if they were so distorted she couldn't make sense of the demons that had surrounded her.

He lowered his head and looked at her but made no apology. "I'm not saying I'm excited about the prospect."

Kendell wondered if she'd been spending too much time with Myles. Her skepticism about Colin's intentions made her consider all options. "How are we to be sure this isn't just another ploy to go up against the loas of the dead? If Myles pulls you to him in Guinee with the cane, we might be playing right into your hands. All you'd need to do is grab the cane, and you'd have everything you wanted. There would be no one to stop you from once again challenging the loas of the dead."

Myles tapped the cane against the concrete walkway in agreement. "And if I did get you to Guinee with the cane, you wouldn't be torn apart. You've made the trip yourself, so you already know that. Your idea is starting to sound a bit fishy."

She'd never seen Colin in less control of his emotions. "Then you come up with a better one, because I'll do whatever it takes to save my daughter."

❧

SANGUINE FLAPPED her wings with Serephine in her arms to get above of the fog. To her surprise, it only extended a few hundred feet from where Kendell, Myles, and Colin had been standing. She kept to the river in case the fog had something to do with Serephine's need for energy.

The girl spread her arms and arched her head back against Sanguine's neck. "I'm flying." Her joy was infectious.

Sanguine remembered the heady exhilaration of first spreading her wings. But she had never experienced the untamed excitement Serephine was feeling. The responsibilities of watching over Colin had always gotten in the way of her unbridled joy of flight. "Where do you want to go?"

"Can I see your home?"

Sanguine spread her wings into a comfortable glide and angled toward the swamp. "You're a lot lighter than my previous passengers. I could stay aloft all day with you in my arms."

"If I stay in this world, can I have wings too?"

Sanguine wondered if that was possible, but she didn't see how. The projection the child relied on for her physical body wasn't a part of Agnes's creation. "I wish you could, little one. I'm afraid you'll have to rely on me to take you for rides."

"Are you my guardian angel?"

She held the small body tighter against her chest. "I suppose I am."

"Good, because I always wanted one." Serephine looked back at the river and flapped her arms each time Sanguine flapped her wings.

Sanguine couldn't remember ever being so happy to be in the air. Flying had proven a useful escape from Colin and a way of seeing the past and looking into possible futures, but never before had it been a pure joy. On seeing her island in the distance, she instinctively kissed the girl's short strawberry-blond hair.

Serephine didn't seem to notice as she pointed to the water below. "Are those alligators?"

Sanguine slowed her flight to just above stalling speed and circled back. "Those are my friends. I call them Lefty and Righty because they stand on either side of me when I need them for protection."

"Cool. Can I pet them?"

Sanguine had never before worried about occupying another creature while in flight. With Serephine in her arms, however, she only dared to touch the mind of Lefty without continuing on to full possession of the beast. *She's my precious child. Protect her with every ounce of your being.*

"I think they'll behave for you." She landed on the bank of the bayou.

The two river monsters climbed out of the water and lay down at a respectful distance from the two humans.

Sanguine had to hurry to keep up with Serephine. "Slow down, child. I said they'd probably be good. How am I going to explain it if you get eaten after we did so much work to save you?"

The small girl looked like little more than a gator treat as she flopped down on her stomach and stared the creatures in the face. "They have such funny-looking big teeth."

"That's because they're from hell. There are lots of monsters out here for my gators to contend with."

The child reached out and touched one of Lefty's razor-sharp incisors.

"Serephine, don't antagonize them. I can see being your guardian angel is going to be a full-time job."

The girl rolled over and sat up to face Sanguine as if turning her back on the monster was no big deal. "I'd like it if you called me Sere. And I'll call you Sangy."

Stop wiggling your way into my heart. "I suppose that would be okay. Are you ready to see my home now?"

"Yes, please." The girl popped up from the ground so fast Sanguine wondered if she had springs in her legs. "Will Lefty and Righty come too?"

"I'm sure they will." Sanguine took the child back in her arms and lunged into the air for the short flight out to the cabin in the trees.

Sere pointed out everything she noticed in the swamp. Sanguine found a new appreciation of the simplest pleasures when seeing them through the girl's eyes. She glided up to the porch and carefully set Sere down where she wouldn't slip off the angled surface. "Sorry for the condition of my cabin. I'm afraid a hurricane relocated it before I was born. It's a challenge doing maintenance with it twenty feet up."

"You live in a tree house!" Sere continued flapping her arms as she ran around the porch. She looked like a little bird exploring her nest.

I guess living in a tree house is actually pretty cool—especially to a child. "When I was your age, I slept on that hammock where the original stairs were."

Sere flapped her arms back to Sanguine. "Who raised you? Did you have a mother and father?"

"I never knew my father, and my mother died when I was born. My grandmother raised me. She's the one who built this whole world. She spent most of her life working on it."

"Do you have any children? I bet they'd have wings too."

Sanguine couldn't stop herself from caressing Sere's soft hair. "I don't. It's just me and the animals out here." *And up until this instant, I thought that was enough.*

Sere clasped her hands behind her back. "I could live with you if you want. I don't have anyone else either."

The tears in Sanguine's eyes made it hard to see. "I'd like that very much, Sere. But first we have to deal with your father."

6

*S*anguine watched Sere sleeping quietly in the porch hammock. The poor child had endured more in one day than many people do in a lifetime. The animals of the bayou sounded as if they were serenading the girl's naptime. *I could spend my life looking after that child. If only the rest of hell would leave us alone.*

But hell wasn't yet hers to command. Like lawyers arguing over the custody of a child during a divorce, Kendell, Myles, and Colin would be discussing what best to do with Sere. Sanguine couldn't take their arrogance a minute longer. She kissed the girl's delicate forehead to get her to wake up. "I have to go back to the city, but you can stay right here. My alligators will protect you."

"You're not going to make me go with you?"

The girl's sleepy voice made Sanguine wish she could cuddle up in the hammock with her. Sanguine caressed the hair out of Sere's eyes. "I'm not going to let them take you from me. This is the safest place for you. If you get scared, think of a bird. One will land right here on this railing. Tell it what you need, and it will come find me."

Sere smiled, further driving love into Sanguine's chest like cupid's arrow. "Is that true, or are you teasing me?"

Sanguine turned toward the trees and closed her eyes. When she opened them again, a flock of white-winged doves had landed on the railing.

Sere clapped her hands in glee. "Can you teach me how to do that?"

Sanguine had never had a stronger desire to impart what she knew. "I'm sure there will be loads we will teach each other, but for now, get some rest. I'll be back before nightfall."

She waited until Sere had closed her eyes and her breathing had deepened before turning away from the domestic bliss of the sleeping child. With a jump off the porch, she was airborne. After the joyous flight out to the swamp, she once again flew like an angel on a mission. She maintained focus on what she wanted but resisted the temptation to fly into that future. *I need to make it happen, not simply escape into that possibility.*

Unlike the river route that she'd taken with Sere, her flight path over the lake into New Orleans created few distractions. The vast expanse of open water seldom displayed any changes except for the weather. So long as the day didn't transition into night, she could be sure she hadn't accidentally allowed her mind to drift her into the past or future. When she came up on the city, however, she had to double-check her sense of time. The sundrenched afternoon she'd left was now as gloomy as twilight after a fire. Though the sun still shone high in the sky, the colors of the city looked as if someone had turned a dimmer switch. Few people wandered the streets, and those who did had the slow, impersonal gait of zombies.

She headed over City Park to the river in hopes that the change was isolated to the Lakeshore neighborhood, but the malaise looked to have infected all of New Orleans. Swooping low over the Mississippi, she came upon the only three people engaged in a lively discussion. From the gesticulations, it was clear Kendell, Myles, and Colin hadn't gotten any closer to a compromise regarding Sere.

Sanguine alighted on the brick walkway of Spanish Plaza but kept her wings spread wide. She needed everyone to know at a gut level that she was the one in charge. "Where are we at?"

Colin looked frantically at her. "Where's my daughter?"

"She's safely out of the way. I'm not subjecting her to a pointless discussion about her future."

With the two men focused on the angelic arrival, only Sanguine caught Kendell's smile.

"So you've decided to be Sere's advocate?" Kendell asked.

Sanguine returned the look of understanding. "More than that. Since her body is merely a projection, she won't be able to return to life, and since she doesn't want anything to do with the loas of the dead, that only leaves one option. I'm staying in this realm to raise her."

Colin wasn't nearly as irate as she'd expected. "Then I'll join you. There's no point in continuing my plan of rescuing souls from Guinee if it takes this much energy just to maintain Serephine's existence. We can be a happy family in a world all our own."

"Fat chance," Myles said. "If you believe we're going to accept that you'll magically change your tune for love, you must think us beyond naïve. You've played that card once too often. Besides, as you said, a death is demanded for both hell and Guinee."

Kendell put her hands up to the two men as if preventing a fistfight. "We've been going over the same ground all afternoon. If Colin is serious about sacrificing himself for his daughter, I say we find a way to make that happen. Clearly, his idea of allowing him to stay here and raise Serephine is delusional."

Sanguine agreed. She considered her relationship with Colin far too tumultuous to be the basis for a long-term partnership. Though he might have some goodness in him somewhere, she didn't think she could raise two children—especially when one had happily considered himself the devil. "All I care about is Sere. Do what you want with Colin, but don't expect me to keep an eye on him every minute of every day."

If he considered the rejection a betrayal, he didn't let on. He turned back to Myles. "So we're back to you having to trust that I mean what I say. Serephine is all that matters to me now."

After hours of talking, Myles still looked ready to resort to fists. "No one gives a damn about what you have to say."

"Clearly," Colin said. "I've been in enough hostile boardrooms to know when the opposition needs to get their story straight. I could stand here for days, debating with you about what's right, but even if we did reach a tentative agreement, unless you agreed among yourselves, there wouldn't be much point to negotiating. When you're ready to talk with a unified message, you can find me in the courtyard behind the club. I believe that's the next gate I'm supposed to approach."

As he headed off down the path along the river, Sanguine wondered what new mischief he was considering. Once Colin was out of range, Kendell turned to her and Myles. "He had a point. We need to figure out what we're doing. All this bickering is pointless. Colin can't leave this dimension without going through our remaining three gates. I'm not even sure the cane would work to move him out of hell because he wasn't cast here from a voodoo spell but from a witch's curse. If Agnes had been around for us to make our case, it seems unlikely that she would have just let him leave without making him follow the rules we laid down. Once out of this hell, Colin ultimately has to go through Guinee to get to the *deep waters*. That has to be our objective."

Myles hadn't turned away from the man, who was now little more than a black coat among the handful of pedestrians. "But if we let him through our gates and back into our reality, what's to stop him from raising holy hell?"

"All I'm saying is, we should look at this one step at a time," Kendell said.

Sanguine knew a little bit more about hell than the other two. "Even though it's the three of us standing guard at the remaining gates, there's no guarantee Colin would make it through. He has to prove himself. This isn't just a matter of holding the doors open. My grandmother's realm has a way of judging the truth. The three of us will honestly have to believe he's changed in order for Agnes to let him pass through the seventh gate."

"And if he does pass," Myles said, "Kendell and I will have to deal with him on our own. I suppose that's only fair. We did leave you in charge while he's been in hell. I won't deny that I'll be more comfortable knowing you and Sere are safely out of his path."

Sanguine knew her next recommendation wasn't going to be popular. "You and Kendell need to return to the land of the living. For you to open your gates, it should be done on that side of the border between life and hell. Since my grandmother left me in charge here, I can stay and still let him through the sixth gate without having to cross over myself."

"No," Kendell said. "We've left you alone too long. We can manage our obligation from this side."

Myles put his hand on her back. "If we try to authorize Colin's passage from the wrong side of the gate, we might end up following him into the unknown, like Baron Samedi sucked into Agnes's hurricane. I'm not losing you again to the insanity of a misaligned portal. Sanguine is right. We have to go back and do this thing correctly. Besides, I'm not chasing this asshole after he crosses the final barrier. If we're among the living, we can be ready and waiting for him."

~

MYLES WISHED he could enjoy the relief of being out of hell and back to the reality he knew, but like a high school student who'd just walked out of class after blowing a test, he knew the consequences of his actions would soon be barreling down on him. "So I guess now we wait for Colin to make his move."

Though they were still on the river path, life—with its throngs of people enjoying the crisp fall afternoon—was easily distinguished from the vacancy of hell.

Kendell pointed along the walkway toward Professor Yates's lab. "So long as we have some time, I'd like a better understanding of what's going on with Sere. While you guys were working on stabilizing the girl's energy, I had the feeling there were things the professor didn't say for fear that Colin was listening in."

"Good thinking. It'd be nice to have something positive to offer Sanguine. I got the impression she'd grown fond of Sere."

Kendell gave him the patronizing look that said, *You're sweet but kind of stupid.* "It's more than just fondness. Those two need each other. From the moment I met Sanguine, I knew there was something missing in her life. At first, I thought it was a romantic partner, but as I've gotten to know her, I've realized her longing had less to do with missing a lover than desiring someone to cherish. Funny how people find each other in the most difficult of situations."

Myles put his free hand around Kendell's waist. "We've had a pretty spectacular adventure ourselves. Assuming we do manage to send Colin into the great beyond, we'll need to figure out what comes after defeating the devil."

She pointed at his cane. "When Papa Ghede gave you that stick, he wasn't talking about a single conflict. My guess is they'll find enough situations that require our help to keep us busy—as if running a club and looking after two dogs weren't enough."

Professor Yates's lab was a hive of activity. Polly was manning the gauges while Lynn, Minerva, and Scraper worked the myriad of dials and levers. The professor was leaning over the diorama and making notes. The pad he was working on looked as if half of the pages had exploded, leaving crumpled-paper shrapnel scattered on the floor.

The professor pointed at Lynn. "Take some more power from the flood-control pumps. I don't want to have to cut any more people out of the realm if we don't have to."

"What's going on?" Myles asked.

The professor kept making notes while he talked. "Hell is collapsing. Since Sere's soul is from Guinee and not our virtual dimension, pumping our paranormal energy into her is like dumping water into leaky bucket. Somebody needs to talk to those damn loas. If we don't plug the hole soon, the World Trade Center is going to start losing its containment fields."

Kendell stared around at the activity as if watching firemen hosing out a burning building. "Just trying to save one little girl is causing all this chaos?"

The lanky professor checked the gauge that indicated the power drain on the abandoned building. "We're dealing with multiple organizations, all working at cross purposes, each with its own agenda. Colin is trying to create his new hell. The loas of the dead think they're maintaining control over Guinee. And Luther and I are attempting to manage our projection from life. We're all struggling with the same power source. Serephine is just caught in the middle."

Myles didn't hear any blaring alarms or the smell of smoke. *Things can't be dire just yet.* "How long can this be maintained?"

"Depends on what you want hell to look like. So far, we've been able to maintain the clocks, but we've had some close calls." He turned his notepad back a couple of pages. "At this rate, I'd guess we've got a week before all hell breaks loose, literally."

"I'll see what I can do." Myles was the only one who could approach the loas of the dead, but he would have to be careful what he said in order to keep Sere safely out of their clutches. He took Kendell's hand. "I'd leave you here to help, but I think you'll be more use at my side."

"Agreed." She turned back to the front door and rushed outside. "Where would be the best place to reach that old fart?"

"I'd say the bank office, but that's not the easiest place to get into. We don't need every loa of the dead knowing what we're up to, so the other gates to Guinee are out as well." Myles led the way toward the club. "I guess we'll have to take our chances in the courtyard. So long as I don't open the portal to hell, Colin shouldn't be a problem. Papa Ghede did say all I'd need to do is set out a rum offering, and one of the loas would show up."

With every step through the Quarter, Myles tried to

figure out what to say—and what not to. The loas would need a reason to help. Presumably, that would be to retrieve the lost soul of Serephine Malveaux. The bait and switch of promising Sere but delivering Colin would only work, however, if Myles didn't outright lie. The loas would detect any untruth. *Please let it be Baron Samedi. At least he has a vested interest in seeing Colin poured into the* deep waters.

Out behind the club, Myles checked the locks on the shutters covering the speakeasy before setting three wrought-iron chairs next to the courtyard table. He carefully poured the rum shots, hoping someone from Guinee would respond. Ever since giving him the cane, the loas had been noticeably missing when he called. For good measure, he also poured an offering over the glowing-green crystal of the cane.

Baron Samedi looked tired as he materialized on the chair, but also much better fed than when he'd left hell. "You have some explaining to do. All we wanted was for you to go to hell and retrieve the soul of Serephine Malveaux. What's with the lightning display? It's like Guinee is in the middle of a dry thunderstorm."

Myles wasn't in the mood to deal with the problems of the dead. "That's why we summoned you. Serephine wasn't in a condition to be returned to Guinee. We needed to stabilize her soul, but the energy we're pouring into her is being syphoned off into your dimension. The hole needs to be plugged to return her to normal."

The loa looked down at his now-empty shot glass. "The problem must be the opening I punched between the realms when I got caught up in Agnes's hurricane. All on her own,

Serephine wouldn't be able to handle that much energy. The power of a single lightning strike would shred the girl's soul to ribbons."

Kendell refilled the dark man's glass. "So if the problem is in hell, how do we fix it?"

"I'm afraid there are other complications. Between my using the bank as the seventh gate to Guinee while designating its office as your fourth gate from hell to life, and Colin's action of pulling Serephine through the gate—not to mention the fact that Agnes dropped me there out of her hurricane—the bank is no longer interdimensionally stable."

Myles gripped the cane, fearful of what the loa might say next. "What, exactly, does that mean?"

"On my side, I'll need to move the seventh gate to Guinee. Before I can do that, however, the bank itself will need to be demolished. That's the only way to free up a gate location. Since it was built in your world, that's where it needs to be destroyed."

Myles looked at Kendell in disbelief. "He's not honestly suggesting we bomb New Orleans Bank and Trust, is he? That's just insane."

Baron Samedi downed another shot, this time joined by Myles. "It's the only way to seal the breach between our three worlds. If the breakdown continues, I can't contain the dead souls in Guinee—though ghosts might be the least of your worries. There are a lot of frightening dimensions out there. Once a rift develops, it can be like trying to pull a loose thread off a sweater. The whole thing can unravel."

Kendell shook her head like a bobblehead doll on a

dashboard after the car had just slammed into a pothole. "Can we at least rely on you to help? Terrorism isn't really part of our job description."

"I'll have my work cut out for me already. If the seventh gate is unstable, I'll need to keep an eye out for wayward souls. Once the new gate is established, it will be a mad dash to replenish the *deep waters*."

Myles continued staring at the empty chair long after Baron Samedi faded back to Guinee. "We're going to jail. Either we're responsible for the apocalypse, or we're labeled terrorists because we blew up a bank, or we fail and suffer both fates. I wouldn't even know how to go about blowing up a building." He looked at Kendell, who appeared equally stunned. "We'd have to warn everyone to get out. This is insane."

"The good news is we could slip Colin in right under the loas' noses."

Myles couldn't believe those words had come from his love. "Sure, no problem. If we're not thrown in some dark pit for the rest of our lives, we'll just take crazy-ass Colin for a little walk through Guinee while they rebuild. How did we get into this mess?"

"If I remember correctly, we bought an antique pipe tool."

He stared at the closed green shutters. "I know Colin is sitting in our alternate dimension, waiting for me to open that hidden bar, but until we take care of Sere, I think I'm happy to let the bastard just sit and stew. I just can't deal with him right now."

He expected a counterargument from Kendell, but she

just sat back with her arms crossed as if watching the devil squirm in the next room. "We don't even have a plan for dealing with the bank. Saving Sere has to be our priority. As you've often told me, one thing at a time."

~

KENDELL WALKED with Myles back to their apartment. The dogs needed to be fed. Even with Polly and the girls checking on the pups, Kendell needed her canine time. "I guess we could talk to Delphine. Maybe there's a voodoo way to make it *look* like we blew up the bank."

Myles walked with such stiff conviction that she could tell her idea of consulting Delphine was a nonstarter. "Since we're dealing with the loas of the dead," he said, "I doubt they'd be fooled by a mere voodoo practitioner. I think we're going to have to research how to actually blow up the building. Joe Cazenave might know about demolitions. He's never been very forthcoming about his paramilitary training, but he's gotten us out of some tough scrapes in the past."

The thought of going through with Baron Samedi's plan made Kendell shake. "Since Joe still works for the police, he might throw our asses in jail just for mentioning the idea. I might do the same thing if I were in his position."

"Or he could provide us cover with the cops. He also has the advantage of being associated with Luther Noire. Surely there must be something left in the World Trade Center's vaults that could pulverize a two-hundred-year-old building."

"Thanks for subtly adding that we'll be destroying a piece of architectural history." She looked down the street at the imposing marble building. "Though it's not like some wonderful event took place there. History might not mind the destruction of Baron Malveaux's seat of power. Sounds like the loas don't have any qualms about losing the structure."

"All they care about is Guinee."

She looked back at Myles. "And what do we care about?"

"At the moment," he said, "saving Sere, but preventing our world from being overrun by monsters isn't a bad mission either. I guess, all things considered, destroying the bank isn't the worse outcome."

She stopped at a coffee shop. The prospect of seeing the dogs pulled at her heart, but saving the world wouldn't wait. "Let's get a cup of coffee."

He looked at her as if she'd lost her mind. "Did you miss the part about risking our necks to prevent the apocalypse? We don't really have time to stop for a latte."

She nodded over her shoulder at the police station. "Step one is contacting Joe. He explained to me that being across the street from his office, this coffee shop is kind of an unofficial way of making contact with him. Lots of confidential informants hang out around the back tables. Just keep the conversation light."

They ordered their drinks and found a table near the front, overlooking the imposing building. "Once this is over," Myles said, "do you think we'll ever hear from Sere and Sanguine again?"

The way the steam rose from his cup reminded Kendell

of the ghost they were trying to save. Losing touch with the swamp witch who was more sister than friend wasn't something she wanted to contemplate. "Hopefully, we won't have to destroy all of our communication network. I'd like to believe I'll still talk to her on a regular basis. I want to watch Sere grow up."

"Do you think they'll ever find their way home?"

His questions made her heart sink to the pit of her stomach, but her sorrow was for herself, not her friend. "I think Sanguine has found the meaning she's always sought. All the pieces of her life's puzzle are put into place by that little girl."

A barista cleaned the empty table next to them. As she walked by, she set a fresh napkin next to Kendell's cup.

Kendell discreetly unfolded the soft white paper and read, "Benches by the ferry terminal in an hour."

She looked around the coffee shop to make sure no one was watching as she stashed the napkin in the pocket of her jeans. "Looks like we'd better get going if we're going to spend some time with the dogs."

7

*M*yles had never been great at cloak-and-dagger. Each time he tried to be secretive about something, he felt the whole world was watching. Kendell didn't make him feel any subtler. She often knew what he was up to even before he did. At least the tourists who walked the riverfront were too busy enjoying the city to be curious about the couple trying too hard to look casual.

"Why does Joe want to meet us out here? I'd have thought some side alley or back room would be more discreet."

"The last time I saw him, he explained that most of New Orleans is under surveillance. Something about the moving water of the river prevents the usual electronic eavesdropping." Kendell found the bench Joe had indicated in his note and sat on the cold metal.

Myles continued to stand, staring across the river. "I can't stop thinking about what Baron Samedi said. It's not just our reality at risk. As if the threat of letting monsters into our world wasn't enough pressure."

She reached out and took his hand to bring him back to the bench. "We can only worry about what's in front of us. Mary can take care of herself. I'd guess every seer is keeping an eye on the future right now. If each dimension is the result of different choices being made, then all we have to deal with is what we're about to do. There must be some version of Kendell and Myles that gets this right. It might as well be us."

Joe walked up with a large coffee and sat next to Myles. "It's about time you two made contact. Luther's going out of his mind. The poor guy is running himself ragged rounding up all the stuff Colin set loose. Now, with the energy drain caused by whatever Professor Yates is doing, the vaults Luther is digging up are proving hard to control. Mind explaining what's going on with the paranormal-power generation plant? If the World Trade Center loses much more capacity to the great beyond, Luther won't be able to keep the artifacts he already has safe, let alone find the rogue vaults. I don't need to tell you the kind of trouble this world will be in if all those magical items are set free."

Such a lengthy speech coming from the usually laconic lieutenant was a testament to the level of the problem. Myles took a sip of his coffee, wishing there was something harder mixed in with the caffeine. "I'm afraid our problem is even worse than Salem's witches getting their brooms back. There's a crack between dimensions, and the only solution we've found is to blow up New Orleans Bank and Trust."

Joe took a long sip of his coffee while staring out at the water. It wasn't until he'd had a second sip that he turned back to Myles. "Does this have to do with the seventh gate to Guinee lining up with your fourth gate to hell? Luther always feared a short between the power lines might be possible."

Kendell held her cup between her knees. "Colin pulled Serephine from Guinee into his hell as she stood guard over the fourth gate."

"That would do it," Joe said. "So now there's a runaway reaction happening between dimensions, and you think blowing up the transfer station will stop the flow?"

Myles was just happy Joe hadn't called for backup the minute they mentioned blowing up the bank. "I know it sounds drastic, but that's why we need your help. Neither Kendell nor I are bomb experts. I wouldn't even know where to start. I do have the cane Baron Samedi gave me, so we can move between dimensions. Maybe we could attack the building from another realm?"

Joe shook his head. "Wouldn't work. The magic in that place isn't confined to the two gates. Margery Laroque relies on an overlapping series of security systems that have been in place for generations. That's why Baron Malveaux moved the seventh gate there in the first place. Marie Laveau promised him voodoo spells to keep the bank safe. In fact, we won't even be able to use electronic equipment without them being disarmed by magic. That means no cell phones, remote detonators, or battery-operated timers. We'll be down to old-school fuses and simple explosives. I do love a challenge. As for the more aggressive security spells Marie cast, I wouldn't even know where to start."

Myles warmed his hand on the hot coffee cup. "Baron Samedi is on board with destroying the seventh gate. He holds himself partially responsible for the breach. Since they're the ones in charge of enforcing Marie's spells, we shouldn't have to worry about demons coming through from the beyond to stop us. Though I guess that won't do much in terms of freeing up electronic equipment."

"Having the lords of voodoo refrain from interfering will help, but that only neutralizes the paranormal aspect of Margery's security system. Since there's so much magical energy imbedded in the very marble of that building, using spells to conduct our operation isn't going to do us any good. So we're talking about a physical act of destruction, and this is where we have to consider the bank's second line of defense. As sister of the chief of police, Margery has access to the most advanced surveillance systems. From the moment someone steps into her building, their picture is sent to a private room in the police station. Within minutes, the bank is aware of everything that's known about their guest. Her security adds new meaning to the phrase *Big brother is watching you.*"

Damn it, Myles thought. Though Joe was a lieutenant in the force, he'd already lost his job once because of their activities. He didn't want to embroil Joe in a scheme that was likely to end in arrest. "That's a pretty impressive security system."

"It is and it isn't. Brother and sister have always presented a united front to the world, no matter the family squabbles or sibling rivalries, but their relationship turned icy when Gerald's nephew, Lincoln Laroque, ingested the essence of Baron Malveaux and became Colin Malveaux."

Myles still had nightmares about being rounded up after his shift at the bar on Bourbon Street to have the situation explained to him by the chief of police himself. "The chief all but had me abducted by his goons not long after that event. Though he'd never admit it publicly, he did express his concerns to me in private about Lincoln becoming Colin. I think the meeting was as much a warning as an encouragement."

"Makes sense," Joe said. "Brother and sister have always respected each other's position of power. But as we know, Colin wants it all. The chief will never risk his position in a direct confrontation with his nephew. It's always more of a chess match than an all-out fight with the Laroques. You'll have to assume every police officer you see is vying for the chief's job. Many of them think Gerald keeps his title through influence and unsavory activities more than reputation and arrests. But having him potentially on our side could prove useful. He might be willing to look the other way if it means bringing his sister down a peg or two and keeping Colin out of the game. Of course, that would be contingent on New Orleans Bank and Trust being able to rebuild. The chief would never accept seeing his sister destroyed."

"We don't want the money," Kendell said. "We just need to demolish the baron's old office. Maybe all we need is a good fire."

As if that would be any easier, Myles thought. "Baron Samedi was pretty clear on his need for the whole building to come down, but the bank vaults must be safe from such an event. Our main concern is that no one gets hurt."

From his seat on the bench, Joe tossed his empty cup into a garbage can ten feet away. "As part of Margery's deal with the force, most of her security guards are off-duty uniformed policemen. If we struck at night and could manage a big enough distraction, we might be able to pull my brothers in blue back to their primary job of protecting the city."

Kendell got up as if stretching her back, a move that made their encounter look like a light discussion rather than three people considering an act of subversion. "Mary hooked me up with the city's homeless population. From the moment they abducted Baron Malveaux while he inhabited Myles's body, every vagrant on the street has kept an eye out for anything that would threaten my safety. If I were to say the word, I'm sure that many unnoticed people could create quite a ruckus."

Joe nodded. "That would give the chief cover to pull the team covering surveillance off the bank's monitors as well, not that there's anything more than a skeleton crew in the IT room at night anyway. With everyone's backs turned, we can set off a smoke alarm in the bank just to ensure no one is left in the building."

Myles got up to join Kendell in her admiration of the

river. "That takes care of everything but the big one. How do we blow up a building that large and substantial? It's not like it's some termite-riddled house ready to fall down on its own. That thing was built like a Roman temple meant to last a thousand years."

"That's why you called me," Joe said. "Give me a few days to put something together. In the meantime, round up your group of miscreants. We're going to need all the help and distractions we can manage."

∼

KENDELL CONTINUED LOOKING at the water as Joe made his way back into the Quarter. "The easiest way to round up the city's homeless would be for me to go talk to Mary. I know she'll be happy to help, so there's not much point in you joining me for the trip across the river."

Myles leaned on the metal handrail beside her. "With the band helping Professor Yates, Joe dealing with Luther Noire and Chief Laroque, and Delphine out of the picture, what should I do?"

She put her hand on his. "Now that we have a plan for the bank, it's time you met with Colin. Just because we have to deal with this gaping hole between dimensions doesn't mean we can turn our backs on him forever. He'll be looking to get through the fifth gate. Just don't get into a fight, because I'm not there to stand in the way."

Myles turned his back on the river. "It's just the two of us now, so you can tell me the truth. Do you really think we should let Colin back here? We convinced him that his plan to save the souls under the loas' watch in Guinee wouldn't work because each person requires so much energy that he'd never be able to bring more than a single spirit across from Guinee to put in one of our puppets. But that was before we knew of the gate-system hole that was responsible for draining Sere's needed power. Once we have this rift repaired, what's to stop him from continuing his pursuit?"

She looked past him to the other side of the river. The ferry was still docked at the Westbank terminal. "I'd say I trust Sanguine to keep him in line, but even she's had trouble preventing him from trying to escape hell. I guess I trust in his love for his daughter—although, like walking on rotted-out boards, I'm hesitant to put too much weight on that feeling."

"Even if his love is true, I'm not sure that's good enough. Look at what we're currently dealing with because of his arrogance. In just trying to save his daughter, he's torn a hole between realities. We can't leave any loose ends. He just grabs onto them and pulls until the whole world unravels."

"Do you have another suggestion?"

He turned toward her. "Now that we're back home and he's still in hell, I could use the cane to pull him through my fifth gate. That should mess up his soul. Then we stash him away somewhere—like one of Luther's vaults—until the bank is destroyed. After that, we kill him, which would toss his soul back into Guinee. If Baron Samedi is right about the loas having to build a new seventh gate, Colin would just be another lost soul in line, waiting to be processed."

"Maybe I shouldn't go across the river. It sounds like you need me to keep you on track."

He shook his head at her attempt to distract him. "Tell me why that wouldn't work."

She held his hands. "Because, my love, it might turn you evil. The whole point of having multiple gates is so that no one judge passes the final sentence. Turn him down if you want, but don't take matters into your own hands."

"And if he makes it through Sanguine and your final gates unscathed, how do we scramble him to fool Guinee into thinking his soul belongs to Sere?"

She suspected part of his desire to deal directly with Colin was to save her and Sanguine from having to pass judgment on Colin. "Just because he pulled others into his hell doesn't mean we can do the same thing."

"But this is what he wants," Myles said. "You said it yourself while we were in hell. If his true desire is to sacrifice his soul for his daughter, then we should let him."

"Sere and I were driven insane by being drawn into hell. What you're suggesting would take Colin out of hell and into life. Even though that's a big dimensional shift, it's not in the demonic direction. His soul might come through just fine. Then we'd be dealing with the devil in our realm again. That is what he believed would happen when he was using the World Trade Center energy to bust out of hell. If he changes at all, it might well be toward his devil persona. Then you'd be standing face-to-face with the devil with only your cane to protect you."

Myles turned back toward the water. "You're saying I'd be giving him exactly what he truly wants as the devil and that his professed desire to save his daughter is only another ruse."

"If we stick to the plan, when he does return to life, it will be as a regular person. We can deal with him as a mere mortal."

Myles wore an expression of frustration on his face. With Colin, it wasn't easy to stay one step ahead. "How about this," he said. "I reject Colin's bid to go through my gate. Honestly, I don't see what he could possibly say that would soften my impression of the devil. But instead of ending his attempt, we encourage him to continue through the final two gates. The system only works if each gate is passed in order."

Kendell hashed out the idea while she gave it some thought. "If we're talking about the gates to Guinee, not going through them in order could rip apart a person's soul. You might be onto something. But he'd have to approach the final two gates on his own. Even though he's agreed to the plan, we can't be seen to influence him toward self-destruction. Sanguine has made it clear that the hell her grandmother built has its own perspective on what is right and what isn't."

"Do you really think he'd hesitate at Sanguine's gate? Do you want me to paint you a picture of how she might test him or what it would mean to let him pass?"

She gave the usual look of irritation. "Stop with the sexual innuendoes."

The ferry was just coming in to the dock. Myles took her

in his arms. "Go talk to Mary. I need to meet with Colin alone. I promise I won't do anything stupid."

She leaned in and kissed him. "For your plan to work, it might be better if you don't tell either me or Sanguine how the meeting goes. I could never lie to her, and if she knows what we're up to, she might not go along. I still suspect she has deeper feelings for the devil than she wants to admit."

MYLES STOOD watch at the railing until Kendell had made it onto the ferry. Then he headed to the club. A part of him still wanted to detour back to their apartment and pick up the walking stick, but the temptation to use it against Colin might too easily create a problem they couldn't contain. He turned onto a city street and heard the ferry horn blast as if it were a reminder from Kendell to stick to the plan.

The shutters that hid the once-forgotten speakeasy were beginning to strain their hinges from so much use. *Hopefully, we won't need you for much longer.* He drew the veve, half hoping Colin wouldn't come.

The man materialized immediately. "It's about time you showed up. I've been sitting here for days. So are we finally going to have this out?" Colin wore his usual suit but with the coat over the back of the chair and the sleeves of his dress shirt rolled up. Myles assumed Colin's more casual look was an attempt to appear more like the common man, but maybe he really had sat waiting in the courtyard for days. Myles smiled at the image of the powerful man sitting for so long like an average Joe waiting his turn at the department of motor vehicles.

He poured himself a shot of rum. If he was to play the role of gatekeeper, he might as well drink like one. "It would appear so." He didn't intend to give Colin any more instruction than necessary.

"I guess I should start by apologizing for taking possession of your body. I could say it was Baron Malveaux, but I've never hidden my actions behind those of others. I'm guilty."

Myles sat in the chair with the bottle of rum within easy reach. "Couldn't care less."

"What?" Colin looked genuinely perplexed. "I thought these little meetings were supposed to be about me making amends for my past sins."

"Nope. I really don't care what you did in the past or even what you do in the future. I'm here because of how and why you do the things you do. Don't forget, I've seen behind your mask. You pride yourself on being calculating and cunning. Here's a surprise for you. You're neither. The way you capitalize on others' weaknesses is similar to a reservoir behind a dam. Eventually, when the wall cracks, the calm, gentle waters of the lake rush out of the fissure and destroy everything downstream."

"And you consider yourself the little Dutch boy with his finger in the dike?"

Myles had no such aspirations. "I'd rather divert the river upstream and let you evaporate to nothingness."

"How do you propose doing that? Because at the

moment, you seem to be leaving the decision-making to the women."

There you are, you bastard. I knew it wouldn't take much coaxing. "They deal with you as they see fit, and they leave me free to do the same. That's why it takes multiple people to decide your fate. You have to win over all of us, but then, you used to run a gate in Guinee, so you already know that."

"I wouldn't have been as accepting of my situation as you seem to be. I ran the seventh gate, so by the time a soul made it to me, there was no higher power for them to appeal to."

Is that how you see it? If I reject you, you'll really just move on, thinking my ruling can be overturned? "Then why bother approaching me at all? You could have gone directly to Kendell."

"I'm not that stupid. She'd never accept my case unless I proved myself with her underlings first. *That* is how the gate system works. You're little more than a district judge, but I have to go through you to be heard by the supreme court."

Myles enjoyed his rum even more, knowing Colin wouldn't be sharing a drink. "And what about Serephine? I thought you were sacrificing your soul for her survival. To me, it sounds like you're just trying to game the system again."

"I'm not here for your cane. I accept that loss. But a person fights for their right to life all the way to the point of death. If I do lose my soul to those damn loas, then I've got Sanguine's word that she'll look after my daughter. But if I can figure out a way to extend my remarkable existence while being able to share it with my child, would you really condemn me for trying?"

Myles couldn't wait to close up the speakeasy. "Like I said earlier: you're like water against the dam. Just know that even if those of us who make up the barrier fail to hold back the water, there will always be defiant rocks left over that will influence the rushing river—even if you manage to succeed, you'll always have me to contend with."

8

---

*B*ack in the apartment, Myles worked his body into the tight-fitting black camouflage outfit. Earlier in the day, Joe had dropped off the thick leotards and packed up a set of their street clothes for after the event. At least no one had bothered asking Myles how his meeting with Colin had gone.

"I trust Joe completely, but I don't see why we have to go on this mission. Seems like his paramilitary force might be better suited."

Kendell tucked her hair into the skintight hoody. "What we're asking him to do is a bit beyond just illegal. If I were in his shoes, I'd be demanding we come along too."

"So we're the sacrificial lambs if this thing goes south?"

She started applying the black face paint. "We are the ones responsible. He's not throwing us under the bus if it is, in fact, our idea. If we do get caught, I fully intend on taking the blame, and I expect you to do the same. Joe and his team are doing us a huge favor."

The neck-to-toe outfit made it hard to breathe. "It's not *just* us. This interdimensional problem has been brewing for a long time."

She held the container of black paste out to him. "I'm just saying we're the generals, not the foot soldiers, when it comes to this campaign."

Just once, it would have been nice to see a war story in which the common guys didn't take all the risks. "When this is over, I'm going to live as boring a life as possible."

"Bullshit. We may not be adrenaline junkies, but when it comes to saving the world, neither of us would shirk the challenge."

He studied her from head to toe. "I don't see an inch of skin. You'll blend into the shadows better that Baron Samedi."

She looked out the French door to the veranda. "Joe picked the perfect night. Not only is there a cloud cover to block out the moon and stars, but the dense fog at street level will also obscure the vision of anyone more than a few feet away."

Myles started applying the thick paste to his skin. "I'm sure that wasn't by accident. What time is it?"

She rolled up the sleeve of the black wrinkle-free fabric and checked the dull-blue face of her military wristwatch. "Eleven forty-three. He said they'd be out front at exactly twelve ten—just enough time to reconsider this plan about a million times."

"Or we could spend the time saying good night to the dogs."

"You mean goodbye," she said.

He performed a series of stretching exercises to make the fabric perfectly coat his body. "Don't be pessimistic. We're headed in with the best, most secretive team I can imagine. And I've watched a ton of spy movies over the last week just to make sure."

Under her black paint, he could make out her look of mockery. "That makes me feel a lot better."

They snuck into the bedroom, trying not to wake the dogs. Both were sleeping peacefully, but they lifted their heads when Myles leaned down over the bed. "You guys be good," he said. "If we're not home by morning, Polly will be by to check on you."

Kendell didn't appear able to say goodbye. He took her around the waist and led her back to the living room. "There's no crying in terrorism."

"Don't try to make me laugh."

He would have kissed her if it hadn't meant messing up her blackened face. "Even if the worst does happen, the band will take in our dogs. They'll be well loved and cared for. Let's get undercover in the alleyway. I don't want to keep Joe waiting."

As they did their best not to be seen, Myles appreciated Joe's unwillingness to discuss the plan's details. Knowing too much would only give him and Kendell too much to fret over. As far as the bombing went, they were just two more sets of hands. Joe was the brains of the operation, and his team members worked so smoothly together that Myles often lost track of which one was performing which task. They could interchange jobs like jugglers who perfectly knew each other's moves.

A black van crept down the street. "That must be him," Myles said.

To Myles's surprise, when the van shut its lights off, so did every street lamp in the Quarter. The sliding door opened, and Joe's voice came from the direction of the van. "Come on. Time to get to work."

Kendell jumped in first. Myles followed so closely he could feel her excitement through his bodysuit. "What's with the blackout?"

Joe secured the door and tapped on the headrest of the driver's seat. "A little surprise from Professor Yates and Luther Noire. They thought with the bank going up in smoke, it might be best if we weren't accidentally projecting energy from life to hell through the misaligned gates. Since they couldn't exactly shut off the projection itself, they figured blacking out the Quarter would be the next best thing."

"I'm glad someone thinks of this stuff," Myles said.

The van sped through the usually busy streets like an emergency vehicle rushing to a crisis. "How did you manage to block off the streets?" Kendell asked.

Joe kept his eyes on the road ahead. "Shutting down traffic in the Quarter really isn't that hard. Now, keep your heads down, and get ready to bolt out the door. Just follow me. We'll be headed for the bank's basement."

The half dozen blocks were the longest of Myles's life.

Yet arriving wasn't any relief. "If I don't have a heart attack, it'll be miracle."

Kendell took his hand and leaned toward the door. The moment it opened, the team rushed out like a football squad taking the field. He barely noticed the walls along the sides of the truck ramp down to the basement. Everything was a background of black with moving black figures pushing him through a black doorway into a black room.

Once inside, Joe arranged everyone against the wall. "One last run-through for good measure. Any second now, our homeless contingent should start their distraction out in the streets. After they begin their ruckus, Myles and Kendell will come with me. We need to start a fire in the old bank manager's office. When the rest of you hear the building's fire alarms, that will be your cue to get the explosives in place. Don't move before you hear the alarms. I don't want anyone caught by some eager-beaver security guard too intent on doing his job to investigate the commotion outside. Five minutes from the alarm, start the fuses. We'll have three minutes from when you light the Primacord to get back to the loading bay. Understood?"

A succession of grunts went up around Myles. He did his best to imitate the sound.

With no lights and no people, the building finally felt like the seventh gate to hell that Myles had seen in horror movies. As they passed through the lobby, he saw outside fires being lit in the streets and windows being smashed. *Kendell said distract, not riot.* But there wasn't much they could do about the homeless contingent at that point. Turning back to the grand staircase, he caught a glint in Kendell's eyes as she too noticed the mayhem going on throughout the Quarter. He wanted to offer her some comfort but, even with Joe's careful planning and assurances, feared any word would be picked up on some hidden microphone.

They skirted along the walls as the fires outside began casting light through the windows. Myles wasn't sure if his eyes had adjusted to the dark or if the ambient light was just strong enough, but either way, he saw Joe raise his hand for the trio to stop.

"Time for you two to do your thing," Joe said. "As this is a paranormal gate, I fear that, even with Samedi's assurances, it might take more than lighter fluid and matches to make this room go up in smoke."

Myles cautiously turned the door handle. Fortunately, it wasn't locked. *Baron Samedi must be expecting us.* He crouched low and snuck into the room, followed closely by Kendell and Joe.

Joe dropped his pack, pulled out a couple of books of matches, and tossed flashlights to Myles and Kendell. "Find something to burn. Other than these sulfur matches, I'm not sure what will work in here."

Myles assumed that the room, being of voodoo origin, had enchantments against what they were about to attempt. *I doubt the fire department has ever seen the inside of this building.* He pulled open the bottom drawers of the desk. "Look at these files. They appear to be the loans Baron Malveaux made that resulted in the borrowers' women being sent to the brothels."

"We don't have time for sightseeing," Joe said. "Spread the pages out on the floor."

Kendell pulled the two drawings from Miss Fleur out of the top drawer. "Should we burn these too?"

Myles didn't consider himself an expert on voodoo. "It might help break the connection Colin has to Serephine."

Joe pulled ledgers from the bookcases and scattered every burnable item on the wood floor. "I'm only soaking this area in lighter fluid. Even with Samedi's assurance that the loas will stay out of our activities tonight, in the seat of Malveaux's power, there's a good possibility that some random voodoo charm will make the chemicals in this accelerant work opposite to what we intended. Those spells rely on what a person is thinking. For example, I can rationalize that I had the matches for lighting a cigarette, so they should still work, but the only reason I can come up with for carrying lighter fluid into a bank office would be arson."

Myles grabbed the hipflask of rum he'd stashed inside the black outfit. "I brought this to call forth Baron Samedi in case we get into trouble. Looks like he'll be getting a flaming libation." Myles sprinkled the expensive alcohol around the room like holy water.

Joe tossed the large boxes of matches to Kendell and Myles. "No need to be shy. Light every match in the box if you have to. We need to get out of here before the riot in the streets makes it impossible to escape."

Kendell lit match after match and tossed the small fires onto every document she could find. "I instructed the homeless to hightail it out of the Quarter as soon as they heard the explosion."

Myles saw the yellowed cover of a file curl at the corners, followed by a blue flame that spread from one cursed loan to the next. "That's only helpful if the riot doesn't get out of control."

Once the fires had crept up the wainscoting on the far side of the room, Joe stood up and nodded. "That should do it. I don't want to get trapped in here. Flashlights off."

The moment Joe opened the door, Myles had a spasm of fear that the flames and smoke would be isolated to the office, but when he heard the alarm blast through the corridors, one fear was replaced by another. *Eight minutes to get our asses out of here. For the love of God, don't trip.*

Between the smoke, noise, emergency escape lights inside, and mayhem outside, Myles began to wonder if they had, in fact, started the apocalypse. Joe led the way down the confusing array of stairs and hallways. More than once, Myles was sure they were going the wrong direction, but he knew better than to think he knew the way out.

When they hit the lobby, he saw men hunched at the corners of the marble-covered room. *If they're still in place, we've got more than three minutes left.* But when he hit the door to the basement, the men got up and raced after them.

Myles had never flown down a flight of stairs so fast in his life. His feet didn't even register each step as he glided over the concrete and steel.

Joe was first out the door, but that was where his leadership ended. "Get in the van. I need to make sure everyone gets out."

Myles held Kendell's hand as they raced up the loading ramp and dove into the back of the black vehicle.

"Get as far forward as you can," the driver called out. "It's going to be a bumpy ride getting out of here."

Myles felt every second pass as he ushered in each member of the team. He didn't realize he was holding his breath until Joe jumped in, pulled the back doors shut, and yelled, "Drive!"

Myles held Kendell tightly as the van swung hard to the right toward the river. He didn't dare look out the window at the screaming and swearing people who must have been diving for cover from the speeding vehicle. A block and a half into the escape, he felt the rumble under the van. The sound of the explosion was remarkably muffled.

"That's it," Joe yelled. "We've only got six minutes before the police and fire departments cordon off the Quarter."

"Don't worry, Boss," the driver yelled. "I'll have us halfway through the Bywater by then."

Kendell was shaking in Myles's arms. "Do you think the dogs are okay?"

"I'm sure they are. We weren't far from the explosion. The apartment is easily four times farther away."

"I'm more concerned about the riots," she said. "If I didn't think I was sending them into a war zone, I'd have Polly and the girls abandon tonight's gig and go check on them."

Joe worked his way to the front of the van with their duffle bag filled with street clothes. "The number one requirement right now is not to change your routine. We'll swing by the Scratchy Dog and let you out. Just throw the clothes over your leotards and wipe the paint off your faces. That should be enough for you to sneak into the bathroom and do a more thorough job before any authorities show up. Your club is far enough away that they may not even bother, but if anyone does ask questions, use last night as your frame of reference. That way, your stories will match up."

Like Kendell could get changed in six blocks in a van traveling at breakneck speed, Myles thought. But to his surprise, when they hit the end of Decatur Street, he was the one still struggling into his tennis shoes while she was wiping the paint off his face.

The van swung around the corner to the side of the club. Instead of heading for the front door, Kendell pulled Myles into the alleyway. "Time to take a page out of Colin's book. If anyone wonders where we were, we can say we snuck out for a make-out session."

"You're considerably more devious than I'd given you credit for."

She peeked out of the dark alley. "With all the commotion, I doubt anyone will have noticed our absence. Of course, the band knows to cover for us."

"I'll tell Charlie to start spiking the drinks," Myles said. "That way, even if the cops do show up, they'll be dealing with a lot of scrambled recollections. And if you happen to have a voodoo spell that would stick us in any video or picture that got shot tonight, I wouldn't object to you pulling out your magic."

"I'll see what I can do. Music works wonders." She did a long inspection of his face. "You'll pass. If anyone notices any paint on you, just say it was soot from the alleyway. Let them draw their own conclusions about what you were doing."

~

AFTER ANOTHER QUICK change into her Olympia Stain outfit in the back room, Kendell snuck onstage and picked up the set list as if she'd been playing all night. The sweat and exhilaration of the night's real activities helped add to the image of the emotionally charged musician. With subtle winks and nods to the rest of the band, she let them know the night had been a success, at least so far.

For the first time in Kendell's musical career, however, onstage was the last place she wanted to be. The dogs might not be in harm's way, but they would certainly be howling at all of the activity on the street, and they had a doggie sense for when she or Myles was in trouble. Then there were the rioters. Kendell knew she was directly responsible for the chaos that was sweeping the Quarter. Her imagination developed detailed images of looting, burning, and fights. All she could do was hope it wasn't as bad as she feared. But most of all, she wanted to find out how well their plan had worked.

Myles was busy with his usual banter and mixology, but from the quick glances he made toward the back courtyard, she knew he was also antsy to check in with Sanguine.

This night must be the longest of my life. Aren't we done with this set yet? She tried to focus on keeping time with the group, but with each new person who entered the club, she looked up, hoping it wasn't the cops. After an hour of dealing with her nerves, Kendell set the guitar back in its stand.

Polly looked all too happy to cut the night short as she stepped up to the microphone. "You'll have to forgive us. We're going to end a song or two early tonight. Watch yourselves on the way home. We're getting reports of unrest in the Quarter. Be safe!"

Charlie helped Myles transfer everyone's drinks into to-go cups. The bartenders weren't exactly rushing people out the door, but with the warning of trouble in the streets, people had an understandable desire to get home as quickly as possible.

Myles ushered the last person out and locked the door. "At least the police never showed up."

Charlie peered down the street before closing the indoor shutters. "From what you told me, I'd guess they're a little busy keeping a lid on things in the Quarter. I'm just glad it didn't boil over onto Frenchmen Street. I can't imagine what the bank must look like."

"I wish I could tell you," Myles said. "We were huddled in the back of the van, so I've got no idea if it's still standing or just a pile of rubble."

Kendell appreciated the speculation, but the boys were taking way too long closing up. "Can we please open the gate to hell now. I need to know how Sere is doing."

Myles put his hand on Charlie's shoulder. "I hate to do this to you, but would you mind hanging out up front? Someone needs to keep an eye out for the cops."

Charlie looked around the room. "Looks like I'm on cleanup duty. Anyone who said being a bar manager was more prestigious than being a lowly bartender never hung around after the doors closed."

The band was already waiting in the courtyard. Polly was fidgeting like a girl expecting bad news from a boyfriend. "We did what we could with Professor Yates to stabilize Sere, but if this didn't work, we'll all need to get back to his lab as soon as possible. His equipment must look like a blinking Mardi Gras float. I don't think that man has slept in five days."

"Right," Myles said as he opened the speakeasy. "I just hope it's not all three of them on the other end of this call. I can't deal with Colin's nonsense at this point."

Kendell had been so busy with the plan and execution of blowing up the bank that she hadn't considered what must have been going on in hell. Sanguine wouldn't have let Sere out of her sight, but that meant Colin would be left on his own, and that was never a comforting thought. "I should have grabbed a drink before coming out here."

Myles set the final shutter of the speakeasy in place and drew the veve. "Here we go—all or nothing."

Sere's young smiling face dominated the image. "I'm cured."

The band sent up a roar of applause, but Kendell knew nothing was that easy. "Is Sanguine there with you?"

Sere stepped away from the gate to show a very tired-looking guardian angel. "I'm here, but it hasn't been easy avoiding Colin. Sere and I have been setting up hiding places outside of the city. One problem seems to inevitably lead to the next, and I figured this was as good a time as any to teach Sere about playing hide-and-seek."

Myles sat next to Kendell. "Let's start with the good news for a change. What's the situation with Sere?"

"You probably know better than I do. We've avoided the Quarter, as Colin was sure to return to his condo when not in search of his daughter, so I can't say how the other projected bodies are faring. There's no longer a cloud around Sere, and as you can see, she is a lot more energetic." Sanguine stepped aside so the team could watch Sere twirling around the courtyard like a helicopter trying to leave the ground.

Polly got out of her chair and leaned in toward the gate. "We were having a hell of a time figuring out how much energy to pump into her. Looks like the settings might still be too high."

Sanguine turned to watch Sere as she transitioned from spirals to somersaults. "If you can provide a dial to ramp up or reduce a child's energy, you might become the savior of every parent, including this one. For the moment, I think hell is stable."

Kendell knew everyone wanted to bask in their success, but leaving Colin to his own devices made it seem as though they were once again playing right into his hands. "Where is Colin?"

"I don't know. Even as an angel, I'm finding it hard to be in two places at once. Keeping on the move has meant we're always hidden from him, but it also means I don't know what he's been up to."

Myles kept his arm around Kendell. "What can we do to help?"

"I could really use a babysitter."

Polly motioned to the band. "Consider it done. We can grab our instruments and give Sere a private concert if she wants. All she'd have to do is promise to stay in the courtyard. We'll even teach her some new dance moves, or maybe she can teach us. All those calisthenics she's doing are making me feel old. Maybe I should talk to Professor Yates about sending some of that energy my way."

Kendell feared she and Myles were once again putting too much on Sanguine's shoulders. "What will you do?" she asked her friend.

"I need to find Colin. Now that we've all but proved that the intense energy drain is not needed for a single person, I'm afraid he'll resort to his previous plan of stealing souls from Guinee."

Myles balled his hand into a fist at Kendell's side. "It does seem like each time we clean up one of his messes, we only show him how to do it right next time."

9

*S*anguine loved watching over Sere, but having Colin in close proximity to his daughter brought out the swamp witch's fiercely protective lioness. She had to keep the two as separated as possible. Once Kendell and the band had headed off to grab their instruments, Sanguine turned around and caught Sere in midsomersault. By spreading her wings, Sanguine turned the potential crash into an airborne pirouette.

"I need to go deal with your father. Promise me you'll stay here. Polly Urethane and the Strippers have agreed to play a set just for you, but I need you to behave. They can't come rushing to help if you get hurt."

Sere held Sanguine tightly around the neck. "I promise."

"I don't know how long I'll be, but remember what I taught you. Think of a bird, and it'll come take your message to me wherever I am."

The way the girl nodded sent waves of strawberry-blond hair into Sanguine's face.

Sanguine lowered Sere to the ground and kissed her forehead. "I'll be back as soon as I can."

Without waiting for a reply that might tug too strongly at her heart and prevent her from leaving, Sanguine flew up and out of the courtyard. *More and more, I am growing to hate the need to deal with you, Mr. Devil.*

She flew in low over the parking lot that surrounded his condo. After three flybys, she realized he wasn't home. *Not a surprise. He's probably investigating how well the seal between the dimensions worked out.*

Flying through the Quarter only confirmed that this wasn't a place for Sere. Since Sanguine's grandmother had designed the buildings in hell, every one of them, including the old bank, looked completely untouched. The wild-eyed people projections with pieces missing, however, were in states of panic. Not one man strolled confidently through the streets as if he owned the place. Colin should have been there. He wasn't the type to hide while observing society's breakdown. *Why aren't you investigating what just happened? Do you even know?*

After an hour of searching every section of the Quarter for Colin, Sanguine flew in a wide circle over the city. *Where the hell did you go?* She made a pass over the club, fearing he might have doubled back to steal his daughter, but the girl was still dancing her heart out in the brick enclosure. In desperation, Sanguine spread her wings and flew as high into the sky as she dared. At the outskirt of the city, she barely made out the long town car headed toward the swamp. *If this is another misdirection, I'll never forgive you.*

In spite of her desire to beat him to her cabin, Sanguine flew over the lake to think. Colin could be headed to her home for only a couple of reasons. A grand gesture of showing up unannounced to profess his love seemed the least likely. She shook her head at the overly romantic thought. A stronger possibility was a move on the sixth gate back to life. She knew he'd met with Myles at the fifth, but neither man had been overly forthcoming with details of the conflict. *He probably thinks I stashed Sere on my island. He must have noticed the change in our puppet people after Kendell and Myles's adventure and assumed I would have wanted the girl as isolated as possible in case things didn't go well.*

She kept a safe distance from the gravel parking lot. If Colin did want to traverse the swamp to her cabin, he could do it on his own. She had no intention of showing him the way. More than one person had gotten lost in the maze of rivers. She settled into a cypress tree to watch his progress.

However, instead of hunting around for her canoe, he casually walked around the lot with his hands in his back pockets, staring out toward the lake. The loud engine noise of an airboat cut the calm like a leaf blower on a Saturday morning. *How is he influencing the projections to do his bidding? This isn't the first time either. I need to remember to talk to Kendell. Someone on her side of the gates must be working for him. Probably that voodoo witch Delphine.*

Once the propeller-driven craft glided up to the dock that extended into the lake, Colin jumped aboard. The shallow-draft hull swung on the water as if skidding on ice.

The pilot aimed the bow to follow Colin's outstretched arm and gunned the engine.

Looks like he knows where he's going. She wasn't sure if she should feel annoyed or flattered that he remembered how to get to her cabin. Either way, her island of seclusion wasn't as covert as it had been.

She took flight and circled the swamp in order to approach her island from the opposite the direction, leaving the airboat to make its way alone. Since apparently she wouldn't get the satisfaction of watching Colin fumble his way through the marshes, there was no point in not beating him to their destination. At least that way he'd still assume Sere was hiding somewhere among the cypress trees and alligator-infested waters. *Let's see how you like being deceived about something important.*

She landed on the cabin's porch shortly before hearing the roar of the engine in the distance. Quickly, she rumpled the hammock and did what she could to make it look as if the cabin had just been vacated by Sere. When the engine stopped its infernal racket, she walked around the porch to watch Colin make his way over the island. He looked ridiculous in his suit. *So this isn't a social call.*

She stood with arms folded and wings flapping in anticipation of a fight. "What are you doing here?"

He stopped a good thirty feet from the tree. "I thought we should talk. A lot has happened in the last couple of days, and I missed you."

But at this range, you're sure to hit me. She squeezed her eyes shut at the bad pun. "What's on your mind?"

He shifted his eyes from the tree to the meadow. "Is Serephine here?"

"She's safe."

He turned back to her. "That's not what I asked. I'd like to see my daughter."

"And give you an opening to abduct her? Not likely. She's just fine where she is."

He walked up to the base of the tree like an expectant suitor. "You're just full of information today."

"I suppose I'm not feeling very chatty. When I see you in your high-powered arrogance, I know you're up to something. Out with it."

He looked even more ludicrous up close. No sane person wore a business suit to the bayou. "Not until you come down. I don't like this feeling of being judged by a self-righteous angel on high who is unwilling to descend to my level."

She uncrossed her arms. "I suppose that's fair." She jumped off the porch and spread her wings for a gentle glide to the ground. "I could use a walk. Talking with you has a tendency to make me edgy."

As they walked along the island's shore, her wings began to settle down. Being at home in her swamp gave Sanguine an inner peace, no matter her companion. She hoped her two alligators swimming in the reeds would make Colin realize his precarious position. "You wanted to talk, so talk."

"I know about the attempt to seal the breach."

One of the few things she admired about Colin was his lack of small talk prior to tackling a big issue.

Conversations with him were like ripping off a bandage even if the gaping wound hadn't yet healed.

He continued. "From what I've seen, wandering around the city, it would appear I've been lied to."

"No one lied to you."

"Then how is it that all of your little puppet people are returning to normal? I thought all the energy from what I created in the World Trade Center was needed to reconcile that one soul to her new body. If Sere really is fine, like you say, and the city is being repopulated with your projected people, the energy required to put one soul in one body must not be as great as you told me."

The fact that he was taking credit for the energy that powered Sere wasn't lost on Sanguine. "We didn't know about the hole between dimensions when we explained her needs. That wasn't a lie—it was a lack of information."

He held his hands behind him as he walked. The impression was of a businessman exploring a building site for his next endeavor. "Either way, now that I know what's actually needed to support a soul from Guinee, I have to reevaluate my original acceptance to your plan involving my self-sacrifice." He turned toward her like a suitor waiting for an answer after a marriage proposal. "My idea could still work, and in spite of your actions, I'd still welcome your partnership."

She couldn't believe what she was hearing. "You were the one who said the loas required a death to balance the living and the *deep waters*. They're not likely to just sit around, waiting for Sere to eventually die again—which according to you would never happen. They're going to come after you if you mess around in their domain. We're still trying to figure out how to pacify the loas of the dead regarding Sere, and you're already talking about stealing more of their protected souls."

"I never said my idea would be easy. I'll still need to confront those bastards. But you did concede that my idea has merit. Any good manager knows to delegate operations when someone else can do it better. With Kendell and her gang dedicated to healing Sere, I can pursue other parts of my plan. And with my daughter on the mend and us in this closed-off realm, you and I could still turn what your grandmother created into a true Garden of Eden."

Hell to paradise with the flick of the fingers. Could that really be possible? "You're like a snake that goes side to side as it slithers in closer to its victim. What if I refuse—will you tack back toward self-sacrifice? And how close do you have to get before you strike and we see your true colors?"

"I'm oddly gratified to see your impression of me hasn't changed in spite of our growing relationship. I'm curious, though. Are you attracted to me because I'm a mystery to you, or is it due to your hatred?"

You think you can see right through me, don't you? She decided not to play into his hands by falling into the trap of confessing her attraction. "You didn't answer my question."

He stood at the edge of the island and looked out toward the city beyond the trees. "By viewing every priority as a starting point for negotiations, I've been able to avoid entanglements that lock me into a path toward disaster. Serephine was the last person I remember honestly caring about before you came along. Now that she's back, I'll do whatever I can to remain with her. So my first goal was to make sure she could exist in this world. Thanks to you and your friends, her life is secured. Giving my life for her seems a little redundant."

"So you don't intend to honor your agreement?"

"Words are like the morning fog. If they don't condense to something tangible, who's to say where the borders were? I left you and your friends to come up with a unified proposal. Even after meeting with Myles, I've yet to see one."

She really wanted to push him into the swamp for her gators to torment. "So basically, you're saying since nothing was in writing, you didn't agree to anything? You must know I'd never accept that."

"What I did agree to was based on facts that proved to be untrue. In light of recent events, I reserve the right to change my mind."

"I'm beginning to understand Myles's mistrust of you," she said. "We acted in good faith. By saving Sere, we completed our end of the arrangement. No one misled you."

"What you all did wasn't for me, but my equivocation isn't because I got what I wanted. You can see the benefit of what I'm proposing, and now you can see that my proof of concept worked. I will admit that I needed a little help, however. Your complaints are nothing more than minor procedural points on how we got here."

She resumed their walk. "They're considerably more than that. Your promise to take Sere's place in the *deep waters* was a noble act. I could have easily loved the man who would accept insanity and self-sacrifice to save his daughter. But the one who reneges on that agreement simply because he can? That man I find offensive."

"So if I'm dead you'd love me, but alive you find me offensive. If that's what you consider romantic, you can have it. Personally, I'd rather live with someone I love rather than cherish a memory. Again, however, you're avoiding my proposal of ruling over paradise."

Her wings started quivering again. "You just don't get it, do you? *Who* I would rule with is just as important as what I'd be ruling over, maybe more so."

"Then we need more time to get to know each other. Now that you're no longer hiding behind mannequins and I've explained my secret plan, I think we're ready to take our relationship to the next level."

Romantic SOB, aren't you? But when it came to emotions, she preferred the practical to the superfluous. "I'll confess to having thoughts about how we'd recreate the passion we had with me sporting these wings."

He looked them over as if they were a new erogenous zone. "I'm willing to be on the bottom, so long as you don't take that as a sign of submission. Just don't go flapping them in the heat of passion. I'd hate to think of what you might strain."

Sanguine went out to the porch to catch the first light of day. Sex with Colin had been insightful, to say the least. *I suppose anytime someone breaks new ground sexually, there's*

bound to be hiccups. We knew the wings were going to be a challenge. I sure made a mess of that room, though.

It wasn't the mechanics of the sexual adventure, however, that had her beating her wings with determined ferocity in the morning chill. Colin had changed during the night. He'd grown more ruthless since their question-and-answer session of the afternoon. Any consideration she might have had regarding his offer had disappeared. Their time in bed had also removed the last vestiges of sympathy she had for his plight regarding his daughter. The man was reckless with people, both physically and emotionally. His blatant disregard for other people's emotions, physical pain, and life challenges wasn't an admirable trait when it came to dealing with their lives. Sex had revealed the true man, and she no longer wanted any part of him.

The sun was still a good half hour from creeping over the horizon. *I need to get back to Sere. I'm sure Colin can order up his Uber airboat to find his way home. I just can't face him this morning.*

Without turning back to the cabin, she jumped into the air and flew toward the city. She hadn't meant to leave the girl alone for so long, but both Sere and the band knew how to reach Sanguine if there'd been a problem. As she flew over the lake, she realized her longing wasn't so much fear for Sere's safety as a desire to hold the girl in her arms again.

The love she felt for Sere had helped her bond with Colin. But where his love for his daughter pushed him toward world domination, all Sanguine wanted was to protect the girl and see her grow into a woman. She angled toward the shore so she could observe the fishermen pushing their boats out for the day on the lake. *Paradise wouldn't be such a bad place to raise a child. Colin at least got that right. But even Eden shouldn't be forced on people. I'll need to remember to let her make her own decisions.*

The future that Sanguine wanted was as clear to her as the expressway that led into the city. She held her body in a tight streamlined posture and focused her insect-inspired future sight on what she needed to do. Each flapping of her wings was calculated to help her find her way back to the exact spot she'd left. *I have to come home to Sere, but I also must know how best to raise her. I don't have to leave her future to chance.*

With her starting time and place mentally tethered to the fishermen, she headed into the future she desired for her soon-to-be-adopted daughter. Not every choice was obvious, and many she thought right proved disastrous later. More than once, she backtracked in time to discover a better answer than what she had first chosen.

After witnessing a lifetime of decisions, she finally traced her path back to the fishermen pushing their boats into the lake. With the future clearly mapped out, she had nothing left to fear. As she flew up to the club on Frenchmen Street, she spread her powerful white wings. *It's so strange to see them once again pristine and feel their youthful strength.*

She settled quietly into the courtyard. Sere lay curled up on a cushion in the open air like a little kitten who'd been playing too hard.

Polly sat watch in the speakeasy gate. "She wanted to

stay up and wait for you, but I'm afraid all the dancing wore her out. Good thing there were six of us. That kid has got a crazy amount of energy."

There are so many futures to keep track of—so many lives Sere will touch. "Thanks for keeping an eye on her." Sanguine knew better than to let on about the future, but that didn't stop her heart from responding forcibly to each member of the family Sere was about to inherit.

"Anytime. We were all glad to have a child to play with. I suspect Sere might have jump-started some motherly hormones in a couple of us."

More than you know.

"How'd the meeting with Colin go?" Polly asked.

That night with him feels like a lifetime ago. Has it really only been a couple of hours? "I know what I have to do and what I've already done. If you happen to see Myles, tell him he was right."

"About what?"

Sanguine so badly wanted to tell everyone about her plan, but that wouldn't line up with what she'd seen. Influencing the future was a sure way of changing its course away from what was desired. "He'll know. I'm taking Sere somewhere safe. No matter what happens, we'll be okay."

endell couldn't remember a longer night in her life. Reluctantly, she'd agreed with Myles that the safest place during the riots was in the club. Playing with the band for only Sere helped, but Kendell kept worrying about the dogs back in the apartment. Once the girl had finally stopped dancing, she faded fast toward sleep, but she refused to move into the club. The band finally decided to take turns at the speakeasy portal to keep an eye on her.

Kendell did realize she'd dozed off, but when Polly's words finally registered in her groggy brain, she sat up onstage and glared at the bandleader. "That's all Sanguine said—'Tell Myles he was right'? And he'd know what she was talking about? Why didn't you wake me?"

"Sanguine was only there for a minute. Sere didn't even wake up. Sanguine just dropped out of the sky, thanked us for watching Sere, and said they were going to be okay and that Myles was right."

She flew into the future. That's the only logical answer. "Did she look any different?"

"You mean from last night? She's an angel living in hell. What's she supposed to look like?"

Kendell realized that it had been a long night for everyone. "Have you even gotten any sleep yet?"

"No, and I'd kill for a cup of coffee. Do you think the streets are safe yet?"

If the riots had spread beyond of the Quarter, Kendell hadn't heard them. She turned to see if Myles had woken up yet. "I suppose it's worth a peek. I'd really like to check on the dogs, but Myles would have a fit if I went into the Quarter without him."

"The coffee shop is only two blocks away. We'll be back before he wakes up. Once we all get a little caffeine in us, it'll be easier to function."

After the adventurous night, Kendell felt uncomfortable walking out the front door without some kind of camouflage. At least she wasn't walking into an armed police lockdown. "So far, so good."

"I'm not sure if that's a good thing or a bad thing," Polly said. "If the bank had crumbled to the ground, I'd expect a lot more activity."

Kendell's nose and eyes burned from the stone dust and smoke that hung low over the street like a fog in the early-morning air. People with scarfs wrapped around their faces scurried along the sidewalk. Fine ash covered the parked cars like a dusting of snow. "I would guess most people are staying inside just in case there are any looters still on the prowl."

"And as a business owner, the possibility of the club being hit doesn't worry you?"

The homeless had their own code of conduct, and typically, that didn't involve breaking into buildings unless there was a dire necessity. "I'm mostly concerned with the dogs, but our apartment isn't the easiest to access. I have to believe the cops will be focusing on rounding up the worst offenders, so hopefully my indigent friends haven't partaken in the looting and are still on the streets. If so, we'll still have our unsuspecting security force."

"Makes me kind of wish the bank vault had been breached," Polly said. "All the real opportunists wouldn't have strayed more than a block from the building."

A rearrangement of the social order was beyond what Kendell had hoped to achieve. Solving the rift between the living, the dead, and the damned seemed enough for one night. "I just hope things have calmed down. New Orleans has enough problems without national coverage of class warfare in the streets." They ducked into a coffee shop with bookshelves lining the walls. "Seems like a hundred years since I was serving up coffee here." The aroma of dark-roasted beans competed with the stench of destruction outside.

Polly stepped up to the barista behind the counter. "We need coffee. A lot of it. Just start filling the biggest cups you've got, and load them into carrying cozies until my friend and I can't hold any more."

Kendell pulled out her credit card with a picture of

Cheesecake scratching her ear. "This is on the Scratchy Dog. Lord knows you guys earned it."

Polly looked at the dude loading the drinks into the cardboard carriers. "Any news on what happened last night?"

He looked as if he hadn't had any sleep either. "It was a madhouse, real postapocalypse shit—fires on every street corner, smashed windows, absolute mayhem. The city wasn't even that bad after Katrina."

Kendell couldn't take not knowing any longer. "We heard rumors the bank got hit."

"Hit? It ain't there no more. I figured you knew. That was the main event. It's like you're asking what happened to that big wooden man after you've left Burning Man."

Polly handed Kendell two of the square carriers loaded with paper cups. "Forgive my friend. We were onstage all night. We're just now getting out of the club."

"Everyone's on edge," the coffee dude said. "I was hanging with friends at a bar on Decatur when it happened. There was this low rumble—not quite like an earthquake but more like feeling a train pass too close. We grabbed our drinks to see what had happened. With all the commotion, it wasn't hard to figure out which building got hit. When we got there, all that was left was the first floor. Everything above that had collapsed into the structure like a controlled demolition. People were climbing over the rubble like ants covering an ant mound, but I don't think they were looking for survivors, if you catch my drift."

"Was there any money?" Kendell didn't really care, but it

seemed like the kind of question someone would ask. She didn't want to draw suspicion.

"Couldn't tell. The cops were pretty fast at forming a human blockade around the building."

Good. That would take every available policeman. It would also explain why no one came knocking on the door last night, asking questions.

Polly picked up her two boxes of coffee cups. "I'll bet the jail is full today."

"I doubt it. The cops were too busy keeping people out of the bank to make many arrests. That's why the looters were so bold. If someone was trying to rob the bank, they did a piss-poor job of it. If it was only a distraction to knock over some other shop in the Quarter, the plan worked brilliantly."

Kendell held up one of the carriers. "Thanks for the coffee and information."

MYLES GROANED as he pushed himself up from the stage. Sleeping on a solid surface made every muscle ache. He smelled the coffee before noticing Kendell handing out cups. "I need that."

She smiled at him as she pulled one of the steaming paper cups from the brown cardboard tray. "Drink up. I want to go see the dogs as soon as you're ready to go."

"How are the conditions on the street?"

She looked tired but less concerned than he would have thought, considering the danger they'd been in. "From what

I heard, the police are busy protecting the bank's assets. If the lawlessness had still been going strong, we'd have seen it spill over onto Frenchmen, and there was no indication of that when Polly and I went for coffee. I'd think the Quarter is probably filled with early-morning gawkers right now."

He struggled to get off the stage. "Sounds like the ideal time for us to blend in with the crowd and find our way home. Did Mary hook you up with any of the homeless ringleaders so we might have someone to give us an update?"

"We thought the less I knew the better. That way, I couldn't give any names if the police came after us. But her people are always keeping an eye on me. Do you think there's some way we could find out if we were successful in sealing the rift? Sere feeling better is a positive sign, but I would like a professional assessment before I get too excited."

The band was slowly showing signs of life, though Charlie still lay passed out on the chairs.

"I'm hesitant to contact the loas," Myles said. "Baron Samedi will probably show up once he feels it's safe. We'll have to watch what we say to keep Sere out of their sights."

"She looked so happy dancing while the band played. It's too bad those who did so much work to restore her will never get to know that little girl. At the very least, I'd like to tell Joe. We never could have taken care of the bank without him. When do you think it'll be safe to approach him?"

"I'd say a year, maybe two." Myles suspected Joe would be in the wind for the foreseeable future. Even with cover from the chief, other detectives would wonder why he wasn't around during the lawlessness of the night.

She frowned at him. "Don't be sarcastic. He really should know that Sere is okay."

I'm not sure I was being sarcastic. He kept that thought to himself. They had enough to worry about without freaking Kendell out about Joe's safety. "Like contacting the loas, I think we're going to have to leave it up to Joe's discretion. We're already on the police's radar. If we go asking about Lieutenant Cazenave, that might tip them off to his involvement in our other activities—and give them reason to suspect us on this one."

"You're probably right. But the two beings I *know* we can tell are Cheesecake and Doughnut Hole."

His legs were stiff, but the coffee was performing its daily magic. "Just don't move too fast."

"Is that because you don't want to draw attention, or are you just not moving very well this morning?" She tossed her cup and grabbed another.

"Well, you are a coffee ahead of me." He grabbed another for the road.

Outside, the smell of soot got worse as they crossed Esplanade. Though there weren't many people so far from the middle of the action, Myles felt a quiet despair as if he'd just entered a cemetery.

"Where are you two headed?"

Myles turned around and saw a uniformed patrolman holding a billy club.

"We live in the Quarter. We're just headed home." Myles

held his hands slightly out from his sides in an attempt to look as nonconfrontational as possible.

"Address?"

He quickly gave the imposing officer their details. "We're just trying to get home, sir."

"You weren't in the Quarter last night?"

Kendell held Myles's hand and stood slightly behind him. "We run the Scratchy Dog on Frenchmen Street. We were there all night. It seemed safer than trying to get through the mayhem."

"And others can vouch for you?"

Myles knew the man was doing his job, but he wondered how many times they'd have to go through the same routine before being reunited with their dogs. "Kendell is the guitarist for Polly Urethane and the Strippers. Most of the band is still at the club. Anyone there will tell you we were there all night." He resisted the urge to let his irritation and lack of sleep get the better of him. At the moment, staying out of jail was the main priority.

"Okay. Be careful walking the streets. There are still a few troublemakers looking for easy prey."

Myles put his hand around Kendell's waist. "Thank you, Officer." Though he had a respectful fear of any authority figure carrying lethal force, he felt a twinge of gratitude for people who kept a lid on potentially dangerous situations. *Maybe it's a feeling of comradery.*

The farther they walked into the Quarter, the more the smell of smoke gave way to the stink of pulverized marble and brick. Particles of stone irritated his eyes. "This must have been hell last night."

"We've been to hell. This was probably worse. What have we done?"

He held her close. "Nothing. We were at the club." He hoped she'd take the hint. If the Quarter had ears before, it would be doubly attentive after what would have looked like a terrorist attack.

She didn't say anything else for the rest of the walk back to their apartment. Each block was worse than the last—scorch marks traced up brick walls, windows were smashed, a few of the openings had been boarded up, and puddles that had been mostly alcoholic now showed the thick redness that indicated blood.

As they approached their apartment building, Myles saw that a homeless couple had set up camp in front of the gate back to the stairs. The man had soot on his face but otherwise looked unaffected by the night's activities. "We stood guard at your place. The dogs were barking, but other than being disturbed by the noise, I think they're okay."

Myles reached into his pocket to offer the couple something for their diligence.

The grubby man stopped him. "There's no need for that. Mary is a friend, and Kendell is the river angel that saved Mary's clan. We look out for each other."

Kendell stepped forward and kissed the man on the cheek. "Thank you for watching our dogs."

Once they were off the street, she started to break down. "What have we done?" Her question was less theoretical and more panicky than it had been just a half mile earlier.

"We saved this world we love. Had we done nothing, what we just saw would have been only the beginning. This city will rebuild itself before you know it. We've seen it endure worse."

She was shaking in his arms. "I know you're right, but I've never felt this much guilt."

He led her up to their apartment. "I prescribe two puppies to make you feel better."

Her smile looked forced, but he accepted it as the best he'd be able to manage from her. When he opened the door, the two dogs bounded off the ottoman and rushed into Myles's and Kendell's arms. What he'd failed to do with words, the pups did with kisses.

MYLES WAS happy to hang around the apartment for the day and rest up from the night before. Out on the veranda, he could feel a tension settle on the city like the fine white marble dust from the bombed-out bank. The city relied on its reputation to attract tourists, and terrorism was never an incentive to visit a place.

Kendell brought out a couple of iced teas. "What are you thinking about?"

He didn't want to tell her he was considering cutting back on the alcohol order for the club. "Just wondering what the projection must look like to Colin. Shit."

"What is it?"

"I suppose it doesn't matter at this point, but our projections rely on these buildings as reality's recording devices. We're back to what Professor Yates was talking about in class years ago about the walls' atoms being the silent observers of what happens in a room."

She shook her head. "What does that have to do with anything?"

"People's experiences are amplified by our drink additives. When those people are out on the street, the buildings capture what's happening, and that's what we send into hell." He waved his hand around the Quarter. "Only now we've put a layer of magical crap over our projectors' lenses."

She set her glass on the table. "Colin knows what we were up to, so you're right—it probably doesn't matter."

Colin wasn't the only person in hell, however. "Sere is living in one of those projected bodies."

"Shit."

"That's what I said."

Kendell tapped on the table. "Sanguine's already picked up Sere. Oh, and Polly said Sanguine said to tell you that you were right. I have no idea what she was talking about. Do you?"

"No, but anytime a woman tells me I was right about something, I usually start checking for what's about to fall out of the sky and land on my head."

"I'm worried that it might have something to do with Colin passing through her sixth gate. And if you say anything sexual, I'm going to punch you."

"Fair enough," Myles said. "Do you think that's why she wanted the babysitters last night—so she could have it out with Colin? I really wish one of us had been able to see her this morning."

Kendell's look of agreement didn't help ease his fears. "I asked Polly how she looked, but Polly had been up all night and was feeling a little snarky. If he did go through Sanguine's gate, then I guess I'd better check in with Delphine. I can't have him bugging her shop just because that's where we hid the totem that represents the final gate back to life."

"Suddenly, I'm less concerned about the bombing last night."

11

*C*olin stumbled through the Quarter, searching for any sign of Sanguine and Serephine. The contents of his stomach sloshed around as if he were on a ship in high seas. Everywhere he looked, he saw his surroundings shifting and distorting. *If this is what I get for having sex with a witch angel, I'm going to use protection next time.*

But his corrupted perceptions paled in comparison to his out-of-control emotions. Sanguine was hiding his daughter, and that alone would have been enough to piss him off, but the blind hatred he experienced violated his basic tenets of self-control. Emotions were power, and losing control of them was a gift to his enemies.

People walked past him with their usual disregard. As virtual projections, they were nothing more than window dressing in his nightmarish world. To prove his point, he took a swing at a passing gentleman who was escorting a ravishing brunette. Instead of the satisfying thud of fist to jaw, however, the momentum swung Colin around in a circle and landed him on the wet pavement.

He remained on the ground while trying to regain some sense of control. His hand ached at having missed its target. In a wild fit of anger, Colin lunged to his feet and tried to tackle the man from behind. Again he landed on the ground —this time facedown and spread-eagle in the gutter.

"I know I hit you." Rolling over, he saw the man and his companion continuing down the street as if Colin didn't even exist.

"Are we back to Sanguine fucking with my perception of the world?" He tried to dust the dirt off his arms, but whatever was coating his skin didn't leave a visual or physical trace. Like pepper spray, the irritant on his body grew more intense with each passing second. Instead of a single burning sensation, Colin felt as if he were wearing a dozen different skins—each suffering from separate ailments.

"This is crazy." The irritation wasn't confined to his exposed skin. He rolled up his pants and searched his legs for some insect bite that might explain his situation. If whatever he was experiencing wasn't from the city's gutters, it must have come from his time in Sanguine's swamp. Hell's bayous would be filled with critters out to make his life miserable. And if he hadn't picked up something from having sex with the witch turned angel, then maybe it had been from her damn insect army.

He gave up on his search for his daughter and headed back to his condo. A good shower was what he needed and maybe a nap. His feet slipped on the wet concrete and asphalt with each step as if he were walking on ice. When he did finally make it to his loft, he stripped off every stitch of clothing and tossed it into the fireplace. The demonic chiggers that were driving him mad were about to suffer a fiery demise. Before heading to the shower, he turned on the gas and lit the flame. "Burn, you little suckers."

The shower he'd longed for felt like hot ash bombarding his skin at high speed. He still didn't see any bites, rashes, or cuts, but the more he tried to relieve the irritation, the worse it got. He rubbed at his skin like a patient at an insane asylum. "This condo isn't any better than outside. It might even be worse. I've gotta get out of here."

He tried on every piece of clothing in his closet, but any touch of fabric to skin created new nightmares. The physical sensations were affecting his thoughts. "This is my body." He resorted to a plush bathrobe as the least physically offensive attire. It fit loose enough not to bind against his skin yet covered him from neck to feet. The galoshes only added to his look of insanity, but they would protect his feet, ankles, and lower legs from whatever was jumping off the pavement to bite him. "Those people out there aren't even real. I should have resorted to wearing whatever I wanted long ago."

With the justification firmly in mind, he headed back outside. No matter how bad Kendell, Sanguine, and their gang of fools made things, he always had one spot they couldn't reach.

He didn't pay any attention to the other pedestrians as he walked along the river path. They weren't real. Nothing was real. In his intense irritation, he wondered if even his feelings for Sanguine had been nothing more than a calculated ploy to keep him in hell. If she felt anything at all for him, she wouldn't be hiding his daughter. She knew what the girl meant to him. Even if the swamp angel didn't want to join him as hell's ruler, she could at least have the decency to let him be with the child he'd worked so hard to free.

The two-mile walk to the grounded pleasure yacht allowed plenty of time for his anger to grow into full-blown rage. He stomped onto the deck and into the wheelhouse. The iron vault was right where he'd left it and still sealed shut. Pricking his finger for the drop of blood that would unlock the door was nearly a relief. At least that was a pain whose source he could identify.

He rushed into the metal closet and pulled the door shut. Though Sere had made a mess of his den when she'd first been introduced to her new body, he'd had plenty of time to put his possessions back in order. The batteries that powered the green light were failing, but they managed to keep him from sitting in complete darkness. Whichever of hell's invisible monsters had been munching on his skin was safely locked outside.

He watched his arm for any sign of the change. Under the green glow, he made out the parallel scratches that crossed his skin like a railway switching yard. "Guess I was a little overly enthusiastic with those fingernails."

Though the prickling and burning of his skin eased off, the same could not be said for his emotions. The need to strike back—even if he couldn't identify the source of the original transgression—continued to dominate his thoughts. He pulled the nearest treasure chest of his old possessions off the shelf. "I used the curse to pull Kendell into my world and the drawings to connect with Sere. No reason to believe I can't figure out someone else to entice into my domain."

He pulled an elegant letter opener from the box. The golden handle was covered in skull engravings. Turning it in his hands, he sought the familiar resonance that accompanied all of his old possessions. The damn object could have come from a thrift store for all the comfort it provided. Though it was a thing of beauty, he tossed it across the small room with such violence that it snapped in half. He pulled out the next item to suffer his wrath—the matching ink pen. He grasped it tightly in his fist, but like the letter opener, there was no return energy. It was as if the failing vault battery was also draining the curse from his items.

In desperation, he pulled down box after box, searching for something that still maintained some vestige of paranormal energy. "How is this even possible?"

He'd been duped. That was the only reasonable explanation. Somehow, while Sanguine distracted him with her ethereal womanly charms, Kendell must have found a way to disarm the curse. "Damn you, witches!"

He struggled to control his emotions so he could think. Even if Kendell had managed to shut down his end of the paranormal connection, she'd never be able to disconnect her essence from the golden guitar pick where she'd stashed her side of the curse. And that little triangle of gold was still in his hell. He rummaged around the vault, collecting the objects he'd recently thrown against every wall. If that pick still had power, there had to be a way to use it to reinvigorate his side of things.

The pockets of his bathrobe drooped from the golden objects. He had to tie the sash tightly around his waist to keep the robe closed. As he snuck out of the vault, he felt like a thief hoping not to set off the guard dogs. The difference, of course, was that these were his possessions, and the guardians he hoped to avoid were whatever microbugs had been munching on his skin.

So long as he stayed close to the river's edge, the feeling of being covered in fire ants wasn't unbearable, but if he moved a block into the Quarter, he was again pawing at his skin like a flea-riddled mangy dog. He pulled his robe tightly around his body and ran the shortest route possible to Scratch and Sniff. *Delphine's shop is an interdimensional embassy, so whatever's after me shouldn't be able to enter.*

He pushed open the door he'd bashed in when he first entered hell. It seemed like a lifetime ago. "I know you're here. You can either materialize, or I'll show myself around."

He headed to the back room without waiting for a reply. If Delphine cared about his activities in hell, or about her possessions, she should have done a better job at securing her voodoo library. The glass-and-wood display case that stood in front of the hidden door to her most precious journals was filled with hideous totems. It didn't take long to find the one he sought. The golden guitar pick, nestled in the square-head nails that were supposed to represent hair, was a dead giveaway. As Baron Malveaux, he'd had the displeasure of having his soul incarcerated in the old African sculpture—not something he was bound to forget.

Without worrying about any secret voodoo alarm system, he opened the case and lifted the totem from its resting place. Instead of heading into the back room filled with so many memories, he set the hated head on the nearest table. "We're going to do things my way this time."

He pulled out all of his old cursed items and sprinkled them around the totem like Mardi Gras favors. The pile of objects looked pathetically small. *In all of hell, this is the best I can do?*

The golden pick showed signs of use at the tip. *The loas gave you all that power, and you just carelessly tossed it into my hell like it was a plastic doubloon thrown from a parade float.*

Cautiously, he touched it with his finger, wondering what new hell he was about to set loose, but like his objects, the pick gave off just as much energy as any other lump of metal. Confused, he picked it out from between the hand-forged nails. "Nothing? Seriously? No bursting into flames, no electric shock, no zapping me into another dimensions— what gives?" He wondered how much of his last few years in hell had been nothing more than his delusions. *Did I really make it back to life? How far gone am I?*

Self-doubt was a mental cancer he'd long since defeated. But as he stood there in his bathrobe, his skin scratched to the point of bleeding, staring at ordinary objects and expecting some kind of magical response, he couldn't help thinking the scene was more befitting of the homeless people living under the freeway than him. "I really have lost my mind."

"Soon maybe, but not just yet." Kendell's voice sent up goose bumps on his irritated skin.

～

KENDELL STOOD in the doorway to the back room with her arms crossed. She glared at Colin across the seventh gate that was represented by the voodoo totem. He was bound to make his case eventually, but she hadn't expected to see him in such a sorry condition. In his bathrobe and clearly nothing else, she wondered if he'd just come from having sex with Sanguine. If so, the witch turned angel really knew how to work a guy over.

"You're really here?" His wild-eyed look of confusion did little to excuse his shabby appearance.

"I'm welcome here in this shop. The question is, what are you doing here?"

He set the golden guitar pick back on top of the totem like a kid who'd gotten caught with his hand in the cookie jar. "What happened to the curse?"

"Seems you and I are just full of questions today. I blew up your precious bank—all those loan documents, personal family histories, and generations of debtors, all up in smoke. Before you landed in hell, you'd been hanging onto your power by dangling that history of indebtedness over every important family in New Orleans. Did you really think the curse only pertained to what you did more than a hundred years ago?"

He picked up a cufflink and inspected it as if he'd never seen it before. "What does that mean for my situation?"

"I suppose it means you're screwed. You started off using these things like a prisoner digging away with spoons at the mortar between the bricks of his jail cell. When that didn't work, you tried playing telephone with me via our connection. Then, of course, you had the bright idea of pulling on the cord to yank me into hell. You must see by now what a complete and utter failure you've been."

He fell more than sat in the chair next to the table. "What do you want from me?"

"Well, that's a change. The only other time I heard you act pliable to another's demands was when your daughter was in trouble. But you haven't even asked about her, so I guess the longing for that possession has passed."

"Her future is no longer in my hands." When he looked back at her, the familiar spark of cunning was back in his eyes. "Of course, that also means I'm not obligated to sacrifice my soul for hers. The loas of the dead are out a soul, and there's nothing they can do about it. And if our connection is truly severed, you're stuck talking to me over your precious seventh gate. All I have to do is leave you standing here waiting, and there isn't a damn thing you could do about it. Hell is mine."

His arrogance, even in his desperate state, was unbelievable.

"Sanguine might have something to say about that."

He tried to sit upright. The movement opened the top of his robe, revealing red scars on his chest. "You started out with a small army. Now you're down to your last warrior goddess—one who's already exposed her weakness for my daughter. I like my odds."

"Then you've given up on your quest for the cane? Just as well, but so long as Sanguine finds you so distasteful, hell will be a lonely place. Though I guess you already know that."

"And what are you going to tell the loas of the dead? They aren't going to sit back and let this situation remain. They're due a soul, and they can't have mine. Do you really think they're going to give your boyfriend a pass for having failed them? Because I've got news for you: the loas don't accept failure. As for Serephine, I fought to the end to save my daughter, but at this point, I think she has stronger advocates. So you and Sanguine are going to have to face me or face the loas of the dead. The choice is yours. I've got all the time in the world." He sounded like an ill-behaved child who'd had a toy taken away and was using bravado to hide his disappointment.

Unfortunately, he had a point. Pulling him through the gate wasn't possible. Both applicant and gatekeeper had to be in agreement. Not that having a half-crazy devil back in life was going to be a picnic, but leaving him in hell also carried too many risks. There was only one answer—the *deep waters*—but for the life of her, Kendell couldn't figure out how to get the cantankerous asshole through the maze. "Do you have a proposal that doesn't result in you becoming the all-powerful devil over every human soul?"

"I know what you have planned. You intend to drive me insane then usher me through the loas' realm like an invalid in order to avoid detection. Instead, let me cross into Guinee without going through your seventh gate. I should have the right to face my fate while standing on my own two feet. Myles can use *his* cane to transport me from here to Baron Samedi's seventh gate. Once I'm in Guinee, I'll no longer be your responsibility. You've ended the curse. Isn't that enough?"

She had seen him make the same play so many times that he'd become predictable. "This hasn't been about the curse for a long time. I may not have wanted the role of protector of humanity, but I'm not going to shirk my duty."

"I'm not asking you to. My plan has the advantage of me not setting foot among the living. Isn't that your number one goal? Taking me directly to Guinee works better for both of us."

Even insane and with his soul ripped to shreds, he would be a threat to the living—perhaps more so. But Guinee wasn't the ultimate destination. "And once you're set loose among the loas?"

"That's my business. I said it before. My promise is to never again return to the land of the living."

She glared at him through the gate. "Then we're back where we started. You want to populate hell with souls you steal from purgatory—or have you moved on to wanting to rule Guinee on your own again?"

"You gave me the respect of presenting my case to you and your fellow gatekeepers. All I'm asking for is the same dignity among the loas of the dead."

She knew better. "Bullshit. You've made it clear you want to take over their realm, not justify your life to the loas like every other member of the recently dead. Papa Ghede doesn't want you back in Guinee. *Our* plan was to get you to the *deep waters* so that the level of human souls you described would balance out. Do you no longer care that the loas might be coming after your daughter?"

"This hell is under the proprietorship of Sanguine Delarosa. The loas can't set foot in here without her approval, and since she's guarding my daughter, she'll never let the death lovers take her. The only way both Serephine and I exist at the same time is if we stay in this hell, where the loas can't get to us, or if I am allowed to deal with the rulers of Guinee." He was like a child bracing himself against his room's doorframe, refusing to go to bed.

"Why are you so paranoid about entering the *deep waters*? Judgment lies in Guinee, and you've already spent time there. Are you really that afraid of bonding with all other souls?"

"I've come too far and learned too much—evolved into a new form of human—to let what I've become go to waste. Even Papa Ghede acknowledges what I've achieved. That's the real reason he doesn't want me back in his kingdom. I'm more than he ever dreamed of becoming."

Your arrogance is unbelievable, but then, I guess that's what it means to be the devil. "You look awfully grubby for being the next thing in human development. You might want to get a second opinion."

"Isn't that what the gates to Guinee are all about? If I can convince the seven loas of the dead that we can be more than we are—and that I can lead the way—they would have no option but to let me live. Think about it: no more death. Tell me that isn't something worthy of mankind's aspiration."

The argument was giving her a headache. "You should

have been a lawyer instead of a businessman, though I doubt that would have kept you out of hell. Since you aren't here to petition passage through my seventh gate, we really have nothing further to discuss. Myles isn't swooping in with his cane to take you out of hell, and I can't pull you through the gate like you did me. We're at an impasse."

He lunged at the totem with fire in his eyes. "Let me out of here!"

On the couch of their apartment, Myles held Doughnut Hole in his lap and ran his hand through the dog's thick black fur while Kendell relayed her conversation with the devil.

"Sounds like Colin," he said. "So we're stuck standing watch until he gives in. Is that the plan?"

"I don't have a plan. His sanity is hanging on by a thread. I hoped that once his mind had gone, he'd be easier to control, but after talking to him, I can see his conniving goes beyond logical thought."

The puppy never tired of having his head rubbed. Myles's hand kept petting. "Colin is obsessed with being alive—not just keeping his soul out of the *deep waters* but also maintaining that soul in a physical body. Maybe Sanguine was right so long ago. What if we kill him?"

Kendell let out a loud sigh. "We've been over this. I can't take a life. Neither can you. And even if we did find

LOVE ME LIKE VOODOO

someone who could, with Colin in hell, he's all but untouchable."

Myles pulled seven dog treats from the jar on the end table and lined them up on the coffee table. "There's something that's been bothering me. So far, Colin has approached five of the gates that we know of and probably Sanguine's as well." He moved the first bone-shaped treat toward Kendell. "He passed Mary's test, but immediately stole you out of her dimension." He moved the treat halfway back to where it had started and moved the second the same distance toward Kendell. "Then he showed up at the club, and Polly mysteriously bumped your elbow, sending the plastic guitar pick into his hand—not really a ringing endorsement from the band." He moved the next two. "Miss Fleur, Antoine, and Serephine all gave their blessings, but he left the drawings that indicated their approval in the bank office, which we've destroyed." Finally, Myles handed the doggie treat that represented his gate to Doughnut Hole. "And I rejected his claim."

"What's your point?"

He scooped up the first four treats and divided them between the two dogs. "If I understood Sanguine's explanation of Agnes's world correctly, the old swamp witch needs to not so much believe what's said as what's felt. If we've all ultimately turned our backs on Colin, then he hasn't actually passed a single gate. He only thinks he has or wants us to believe he has."

Kendell nodded toward the remaining two treats. "And what about Sanguine?"

"She's taken Sere and flown off to some unknown part

of hell. That doesn't seem like the act of someone who's granted forgiveness."

"I still don't see your point. What use are the gates if he doesn't intend to work with us?"

He gave the remaining two treats to Cheesecake. "Assume we let him sneak out of hell. You know how confused you were when you made it out of his vault? Multiply that times seven. All of the devil's cunning won't do him any good if he's nothing more than a crazed homeless person. Without support, an indigent madman claiming to be the devil isn't going to intimidate anyone. The bank is in shambles, so his mother isn't likely to reach out to him. Chief Laroque doesn't give a rat's ass about his nephew. Who's he going to turn to?"

Kendell sat on the floor to pet Cheesecake. "And if he did go through the gates, even if we all rejected him later, you're banking on him not having any devilish magic up his sleeve?"

"Sanguine didn't get to keep her wings when she returned, and her ability to read the future wasn't any more prophetic than that of any other seer. What she had achieved in hell remained in hell. I know it's a risk letting Colin back into our world, but no matter which calendar we're using, he can't return as a young man. Messing with time as much as he has while in Agnes's realm must have taken a toll. He only gets to modify his appearance while in that other dimension. Once he's back here, he might not have many years to live, in addition to no friends or allies, no home, and none of the loans he used as leverage over the rich and powerful. Take away any magical powers, and he's in worse shape than your homeless contingent. Might do the bastard good to see life from the other side of the socioeconomic scale."

She shook her head. "That still doesn't do us any good regarding Sere. By the time he dies, the loas will know it's Colin. The window of opportunity to sneak him through their seventh gate undetected while they're rebuilding won't last long."

"Which brings me back to my original point. He has to die. At least being in our dimension makes finding an assassin somewhat easier. And if no one is supporting him, the loss of his life may go unnoticed by the authorities."

She stared down the hallway and frowned. "Hypothetically, even if he did come back to life and—again hypothetically—we did kill him, you'd still need to escort his soul through Guinee to the seventh gate. He might not be much in this realm, but once his soul is set free of his body, he'd be an out-of-control lunatic."

"True, and I can't believe I'm saying this, but I suspect Delphine might have a constraining harness we could put on his soul like a muzzle on a rabid dog."

She gave him the usual tilted-head expression of self-satisfaction. "So you're easing up on your opinion of Delphine?"

Not likely. "Once Colin is returned to life, crazed, and someone finally kills him, she won't have much choice but to help us dispose of the evidence. She does bear more than a little responsibility for creating Colin. If we're right about her, approached correctly, she might see that she's been backing a losing cause with him. And what better way to honor her ancestor than to draw to a close the evil Marie Laveau let loose?"

"We still have the problem of getting Colin to pass through the seventh gate. He knows what we're up to. Why would he want to sneak through?"

Myles hitched his thumb down the hallway. "We make the cane an irresistible target. He won't approach the gate if he thinks you're standing guard, but if he believes he can win it all while we're not looking—doesn't that sound like something Colin would think up himself?"

"We'll need a powerful backup plan if he does get hold of the cane. We could be playing right into his hands."

"We do have a pretty good crew," Myles said. "The real question will be how best to utilize them."

"And how to tempt Colin into trying to steal the cane. We can't be too obvious, or he'll be suspicious."

Myles walked down the hallway to the closet. "So I can't just leave the cane next to the gate like I'd misplaced it?"

"Right. But it will need to be somewhere he'd notice it."

Instead of pulling out the cane, Myles grabbed the silver headpiece. "We've long suspected he's had help from this side. Our guess has been Delphine. What if we ask her to hold this for us? She keeps every other magical token in her voodoo curio cabinet, so why not this one as well? From what you described, it sounds like Colin set his statue facing the others. If he was looking through the totem as the seventh gate and saw the silver headpiece in the cabinet, he might think it was a sign from Delphine."

"Suddenly, you're putting a lot of trust in that voodoo queen. What if she actually does use it as a sign to Colin?"

He pulled out the cane. "We won't tell her where to find the cane, and I'm certainly not leaving it here in the apartment."

"We'd still be connecting Colin to Delphine."

Myles wasn't crazy about having to face both the devil and the voodoo queen, but Delphine had proven ineffectual enough times for him to doubt her abilities. "When you were half out of your mind, Delphine didn't have much useful information on how to cure you. Polly was the one who figured out that the band needed to utilize your musical magic. If Delphine can't cure him of his interdimensional insanity, he might be so out of his mind that he wouldn't even realize she was on his side."

"And there is always the possibility she could help us without having any ulterior motive," Kendell said.

We never are going to see eye to eye on that woman. "If she doesn't help Colin, all the better. But if she tries, she'll be in for a challenge that so far has been beyond her skill set. Without the cane, even I wouldn't know how to cure him. It was one hell of a task getting Sere straightened out."

MYLES DIDN'T like keeping anything secret from Kendell, not that he ever could. She had an almost sixth sense about whether he was hiding some bit of information. But they both agreed it would be better if she didn't know where he hid the cane. After all, she had to deal with Delphine on her own if their plan was to stand a chance, and the less he knew about what was said, the less likely he was to form new suspicions regarding the voodoo queen. If what he didn't know didn't hurt him, the same should be true regarding her lack of knowledge about what he did with the cane.

Of course, that meant *he* needed to figure out what to do with the damn stick. The most obvious places all carried potential risks. Professor Yates was too well connected with Luther Noire to be trusted with such a powerful paranormal item. Even if the professor didn't mean to, he could easily let the information slip when speaking to the collector of magical artifacts. Then it'd be an all-out war to get it out of the World Trade Center vaults. Polly and the band were out. Like Myles, they never could keep a secret from Kendell. The people in the interdimensional embassies would be drooling to get their hands on the cane, so that removed those buildings as potential hiding places.

Myles walked down Frenchmen Street, rejecting option after option. In front of the club, Charlie was busy unloading his truck filled with cases of alcohol. At least the business was in good hands, even if the cane wasn't. Myles stood still, considering the opportunity in front of him.

"You going to help me unload these boxes, or just stand there like a statue?" Charlie yelled from inside the back of his truck.

"Just let me stash this stick in the cab. Don't want anyone walking off with it."

Charlie stood upright with a case of Jameson's in his hands. "I don't usually see you carrying that thing around unless there's a problem. Should I be expecting another wild night? Because if so, I'm stashing one of these crates in the back for employee use."

Myles grabbed the nearest crate of Jack Daniels "Actually, I need a favor. Think you can hide that stupid stick somewhere no one would find it?"

"Including you? If you're on the voodoo wagon, I'll be your twelve-step sponsor. Or is it seven steps?"

"I wish." The manual labor of carrying boxes felt good. It reminded Myles of their bartending days in the Quarter when his chief job had been doing whatever Charlie instructed. "We're running a game of deception, and we need to convince the devil to come play. You'll have to hide the cane someplace close. When I do need it, I'll be in a hurry."

Charlie gave him the usual scowl of disapproval. "I'm certain I don't want to know the details. How long of a head start does this fox have before you release the hound?"

"I don't want you anywhere near that thing when Colin comes hunting for it. Kendell's talking to Delphine before heading to the club. Once she has the trap baited, it's anyone's guess on how long it will take Colin to notice, but he's never been one to let an opportunity sit idle for long."

Charlie put the last case on the bar. "Then I guess it'll be up to you to set up for tonight. That'll give me three hours to find a haystack to hide your needle in before opening the club."

Myles watched Charlie drive off, hoping he hadn't just put his friend in mortal danger.

~

KENDELL STRUGGLED with how much to confide in Delphine. Myles's suspicions about the voodoo practitioner had proven right far more often than not. The one thing they both could agree on, however, was Delphine's dedication to the reputation of Marie Laveau.

She pushed open the door to the shop with a feeling of dread. *Why couldn't this have been the building that needed to be burned down?*

"Are you here to see me, or just passing through again?" Delphine didn't stop organizing her fragrances.

Kendell pulled the silver skull from her bag. "I need to get this headpiece out of the apartment. Having it so close to the cane is raising enough paranormal energy to give me a headache. I was hoping you could hang onto it for me."

Delphine stopped playing with her dark-brown jars. "What mischief has the devil been up to this time?"

Of course you'd see through me. "For a change, we thought it might be fun to lead him on for a while."

The voodoo expert took the silver skull and turned it in the light. It seemed to glow in the woman's brown fingers. "And what do you want me to do with it?"

"Stick it in your cabinet with the other totems. It is an artifact from Marie Laveau after all. It belongs in your collection."

Delphine squeezed it in her hand as if trying to crush it. "Don't bullshit me. What do you expect to happen?"

No use in lying. Either you're with us, or you're not. "Colin won't come through the seventh gate the way we'd like, so we thought we'd provide a little incentive."

Delphine stopped playing with the trinket. "This is

Myles's idea, isn't it? Sounds like the kind of foolhardy ploy he'd come up with. I assume Colin has already worked through all of the other gates?"

"He's presented his case to each guardian, including me."

The woman sat in the chair behind her worktable. "I won't ask if you've all accepted his pleas, just as I don't want to know your scheme for him once he shows up. I'll take the trinket, but leave me out of whatever you've got planned."

Like you're some innocent bystander? But Kendell knew Delphine's ignorance was in everyone's best interest. "Just stash it as a favor to me. And if Colin should happen by, I wouldn't mind a heads-up."

"I'm only doing this because Marie put a spell on this headpiece."

13

*E*ach day for Colin was worse than the last. Hives covered every exposed area of skin. The itching was intolerable. Being in the vault helped only slightly, but hiding never won a war. In an act of supreme self-will, he abandoned the comfort of the iron walls and returned to his condo. He still needed to go back on the offensive. His mind, however, was as consumed with the scratching as his fingers.

He gave up on his wardrobe. The bathrobe was all he could stand next to his skin. *Think, damn it. How do I get out of this mess?* Pacing from one wall to the next, he'd measured out the condominium too many times to count. What had been a luxury penthouse now felt like a cage. Looking outside, however, made his skin crawl. If he was to leave the relative safety of the brick walls, he needed a specific destination and a plan.

Each window displayed a different frustration. He didn't

need the view of the World Trade Center to know he'd never make it back into the vaults. Luther had turned the building into a fortress. With only Colin to worry about, the guardian of the paranormal had been able to custom design a security system for the only inhabitant in hell. The next wall of windows presented Colin with the bank and police station. *Like either my mother or uncle would give a damn about my situation.* Staring downriver toward his vault was the most depressing of directions. Now that the curse had been broken, he had no way of powering up the cabinet. Even the river seemed to mock him with its continuous flow toward the gulf, as if to say, "Even I can escape hell."

He grew dizzy from circling the penthouse. Sanguine and Serephine had left, disappearing over some horizon without leaving him any hint of how to reach them. The gatekeepers had all fulfilled their duties as they saw fit. Only Kendell might still meet with him, and she wasn't likely to talk with him unless he first bowed down and kissed her feet.

Her inattention is an advantage. He stood still to let the thought fully form. Like Sanguine after having sex, Kendell would have her back turned to him. She wouldn't be hanging out at the voodoo perfumery, waiting for him. Delphine, however, never left the premises. Her assistance wasn't assured, but she had secretly made it possible for him to interact with the puppets that filled his reality. As he stared out into the Quarter, his adrenaline started combating his irritation—both mental and physical. *Contacting that voodoo witch is at least worth a try. Anything is better than pacing this damn cage.*

Though the galoshes hurt going on, they provided the right amount of protection while leaving enough room for his swollen feet and ankles. He caught himself in the mirror: hair disheveled, skin covered in welts and scratches, bathrobe caked in the Quarter's slop, and mud boots to complete the look of a homeless person in need of psychiatric help. "At least I won't get mugged." The pathetic joke made him laugh so hard he had to hold his stomach. The cackling hurt his ears, but he found it impossible to stop.

He forced his way out of the condo, hoping the change of scenery would distract his mind from its off-handed attempt at humor. *Right. No more jokes.*

Walking along the streets felt like being pelted with lava. The human projections had become more substantial, but even they had confused looks on their faces. Each person he passed was like an actor in a play who'd forgotten his or her lines. He had no sympathy for any of them. Whatever they were experiencing, at least they could still function.

Colin kept his hands in the pockets of his robe and busted open the door to Scratch and Sniff with his shoulder. At midafternoon, the place was deserted. Delphine didn't usually wander over from the other side of the shotgun double until dusk. In the back room, he fell into the chair to wait for her.

He stared at the voodoo totem he'd pulled out of the case. Its horrendous sewn-shut leather eyes and mouth made him wonder what the statue would say about his predicament if it could talk. "Have I mentioned how much I hated being stuck in you?"

Though Delphine's shop provided no more protection than his condo, at least it was a change of scenery. "I have to get out of this hell. They've left me no other choice. Without power and the cane, I can't turn this place into a realm for immortals. And this itching will drive me even more mad than I presently am." His head drooped to the side. Looking past the wooden head, he saw all the other totems in the case. "I wonder how many other devils…"

The glint of light from the small silver skull made him catch his breath. *That can't be possible. Are my jailors really that foolish?*

He got out of the chair without taking his eyes off the small headpiece nestled behind the much larger totems. The cabinet door swung open with barely a touch as if inviting him to take what he wanted.

His hand shook as he reached between the wooden heads to the silver skull. He lifted it free of the shelf. "No security system at all?" For a second, he suspected he was being set up, but this wasn't the first time he'd borrowed something from Scratch and Sniff without any negative outcome. His consequence-free snagging of her totems for use in creating the World Trade Center paranormal power plant had proven that Delphine would turn a blind eye to his activities. He turned in his hand the hollow skull made of beaten pieces of eight. It was a welcome reminder of his life as Baron Malveaux, his hundred years in Guinee, and his brief return in the living in the body of Myles Garrison. "I'd know you in any dimension. The question is, where's your cane?"

If it was in hell, the skull would lead him to it. Even

better, if it was still among the living, he could use the connection to pass back into the realm of real people. Colin turned to the shop entrance in the next room and wondered if it really could be that simple.

He walked through the shop, skull in hand, and cautiously opened the front door, anticipating some new nightmare. Very little appeared different than the street he'd escaped. He took a deep breath of the cool air. It didn't burn his nose, throat, and lungs as it had when he'd entered the building. Heartened by the first success, he left the shop. People looked at him out of the corners of their eyes as they passed by. After all the time he'd spent not being noticed, the secretive glances were like spotlights.

"What, you've never seen a man in a bathrobe before?" Yelling only made the pedestrians hurry faster down the sidewalk. Their fear of him threatened to restart his out-of-control laughter.

This could just as easily be another delusion. Kendell and Sanguine do love putting on their little plays. Only one way to be sure. He stiffened his bent fingers and took a swipe at a woman passing by, like a cat trying to scratch an unsuspecting guest walking down the family's hallway. He missed.

"Freak." The woman ran across the street as fast as her fashionable shoes would allow.

A heavyset college-aged dude in a Saints T-shirt took Colin's arm. "Hey, buddy, do we need to get you some help?"

Colin tried to bite the hand, but it was too far away. "I need to taste your blood. Just a drop would do. I promise I'm not crazy."

"Of course you're not. It's perfectly normal to act like a homeless vampire in New Orleans. Now, why don't you let me help you find your lair."

"I'm not a fucking vampire." But as Colin thought about explaining how he was the devil just escaped from hell and only wanted a taste of blood to confirm he'd returned to life, he wondered if accepting the title of vampire might be more believable.

The young man let go of Colin's arm. "Hey, I'm just trying to help. We've all been on bad trips before, old man."

"Who are you calling old? Do you know who I am?" But with a glance at his freed arm, Colin noticed his skin wasn't as tight and supple as he remembered. Wrinkled, splotchy, and more gray than pink, his flesh looked like that of his grandparents. The muscular dude's handprint where he'd grabbed Colin's arm was an anemic white.

"Dude, just sleep it off, okay? I don't want to have to call the cops on you, but if you try to take a bite out of someone else, you're not going to leave me any choice. And you might want to find a better place to hang out. Delphine de Galpion doesn't like bums sleeping on her doorstep. Most of your people hang out under the freeway overpass."

Colin pulled his bathrobe tighter around his body. "I'm not homeless."

"That's good. Let me call you a cab so they can take you home. I'm sure someone must be pretty worried about you right now. Did you sleep in the gutter last night?"

This guy is really getting on my nerves. "Look, I'll be fine."

But once the Good Samaritan left and Colin no longer had his anger to focus on, everything started spinning. He fell against the shuttered window of Delphine's shop and passed out.

~

WHEN COLIN CAME TO, he found himself bound to a chair with Delphine holding a sword to his chest. *At least it isn't flaming.* "What do you think you're doing?" he asked.

She pressed the tip between the lapels of his bathrobe and drew a spot of blood. "First, making sure it's really you. You've aged."

"So I've been told. Mind taking the point of that blade out of my chest?"

She twisted the tip. "For now, we'll keep things as they are. That includes the skull in your pocket."

He could feel the lump of silver pulling at his bathrobe. "What does that have to do with anything?"

"Haven't you wondered why you're still relatively clearheaded? Once I take that bobble from you, this reality is going to make your hell look like a playground. The connection to the cane is all that's allowing you to hold on to the last of your sanity."

Even with the threat of death at his chest, he breathed a little easier. "I suppose I should thank you for leaving it for me. Now, how are we going to go about getting the cane?"

She pressed the tip deeper into his skin. "You really are incredible. Do you honestly believe I had anything to do with letting you out of hell?"

"Stop playing with me. Of course you put the silver skull

in your curio cabinet for me to use. Who else could have done it, and why?"

She frowned at him and didn't answer, as if expecting him to figure it out on his own.

The answer can't be that obvious. "Why would Myles want me back among the living? He made it clear that this is the last place he wants me." Colin looked around to see if there was anyone else in the room. "If it was Myles, Kendell, or any of their gang of idiots, they didn't do a very good job. Now, get me out of these ropes so we can get to work."

She eased the sword out of his flesh but kept it aimed at his heart. "I told you from the beginning, my allegiance is to Marie Laveau and her alone."

"Fine, but my money has come in awfully handy to you in the past." With Delphine, it was always a matter of spinning his plan to make Madam Laveau look like the ultimate mastermind. "Once I've got the cane back, I'll defeat the loas of the dead. Isn't that what Marie wanted all along—to take our fate into our own hands?"

She didn't break eye contact as she leaned in and took the silver headpiece from his pocket. "Why don't you ask her yourself?"

As she plunged the sword into his chest, Colin's consciousness melded with his blood. He felt the thick life force drain from his heart, run down the length of the blade, enter the totem's mouth at his back, fall down the hollow wooden throat, and finally, fill the spirit jar in its stomach.

"No!" But the word only echoed in his being without finding an outlet.

The sticky black tar walls, smell of rotting flesh mixed

with rum, and overwhelming despair hadn't changed much from when he'd been condemned to the totem as Baron Malveaux. *This is the second time that voodoo witch has cast me into this fetish, but she's clearly not skilled enough to have created it.*

"Where are you, old witch? You must be here somewhere. Delphine never made a threat she couldn't keep." His prison cell transformed into an elegant parlor. He didn't need any introduction to the woman in African dress who sat on the throne in the middle of the room. "It's been a long time. Mind explaining what I'm doing back here?"

Marie Laveau had the same aura of regal authority he remembered from his days as Baron Malveaux. "Righting a wrong I committed long ago. You were never supposed to have that cane. The prophecies weren't about you. Even I didn't always read the signs correctly. My arrogance prevented you from getting the death you deserved. Then the loas got involved. The whole ugly affair has haunted me ever since. I set this totem up for the day I knew we'd meet so I could explain the situation. Looks like my patience has finally paid off."

For all of the enshrined history about the voodoo queen, Colin had always found her more down-to-earth than any religious person he'd met. "So what's your plan now that you have me? Please don't say you're just going to turn me over to the loas of the dead. That doesn't sound very sporting."

"*I'm* not going to do anything," she said. "My time has passed. Someone needed to set you straight on Baron Samedi's cane. You keep thinking all you have to do is gain possession and the powers will be yours. Even in the short time that Myles Garrison has had it, you must have noticed how much better he is with it than you ever were. The cane is only a symbol of power, not the power itself. No matter what you do, you'll never have the command of the staff that you envision. Magic doesn't reside within an object. A thing only manifests what's inside a person's soul, like a magnifying glass focusing light into a burning point. You need to have the correct energy source matched up with the right lens. You and the cane were never a good fit. Perhaps that's what drove you to evil. For my part in that history, I'm sorry."

Please tell me I don't have to spend eternity listening to her pontificate about my failures. "Seems like you could have found an easier way of conveying the message without resorting to Delphine committing murder."

She shrugged as if to say such things as life and death didn't matter. "You're not the easiest person to convince."

Kendell paced the apartment with Cheesecake keeping a watchful eye from the ottoman. "It's been a week with no word from Delphine. Even Colin isn't that stupid. He must have made some attempt at escape by now."

Myles entered from the kitchen and handed her a beer. "If he were loose on the streets, we'd have heard about it. Any word from the homeless contingent?"

"Nothing useful. My friends heard about a tourist running down Royal, yelling that some crazy guy was trying to bite her, but since it was just that one woman, they suspected something nefarious had been added to her drink."

Myles twisted off the top to the bottle in his hand and traded with her. "Each night, I've kept a watchful eye at the club. If he did make it out of hell, even out of his mind, I'd expect him to stumble into the Scratchy Dog at some point. Your music would draw him in no matter his condition."

She blushed at the compliment. "What can I say? I've got a way with the bad boys."

"Some of the good ones too." He kissed her on the cheek. "Seems like we're getting a little short on ways to check in with hell, especially with Sanguine off playing foster mother to Sere. I wish she'd at least try to check in to let us know they're okay. She didn't even say goodbye."

"Don't give me something else to worry about," Kendell said. "I fully intend to give Sanguine a piece of my mind when she resurfaces, but I believe she's okay. If there was a problem, I'm sure we'd have heard. My guess is she's just keeping Sere away from her father. No girl should see her dad lose his mind, not even the devil's daughter."

Myles took a long swig of his beer. "We could check in with Professor Yates. He often comes up with ideas I hadn't considered."

"Other than showing us what the projected mannequins are up to, I don't see how he'd be much use in finding Colin."

"He was able to figure out what Colin was up to by tracing how he'd interacted with our puppets, but if Colin has gone into hiding, that won't do us much good."

Kendell resumed her pacing. "We don't dare go into hell to search for him. If he is playing his games again, he might be waiting to ambush us so he can try once more for your cane. I don't see any more moves."

Myles set his empty bottle on the coffee table. "Let's assume for a moment that Colin isn't sitting idle in hell, waiting for us to make a move. That doesn't sound like him anyway."

"Sure, but if he came through the gate, we'd have seen him. We're back where we started."

He shook his head. "Not if he's unable to leave Scratch and Sniff."

She could see in his eyes where his thoughts were taking him. "You think Delphine has him? I'm not sure she could hold him even if she wanted to. He'll be out of his mind. Unless she put a binding spell on him, she'd never be able to control him. And why would she hold him captive?"

"I didn't say she was working against him. If she were, she'd have contacted us."

Some first impressions never change. "I can't accept that she would agree with his plan of dominating all human spirits. It goes against everything the loas of the dead believe in. She might not always agree with Papa Ghede, but he is pretty much the head of her religion."

"Colin can be pretty persuasive."

Myles still held concerns about Colin's advances toward Kendell, but he didn't know just how far the man had fallen. "When he's at the top of his game, he can make a compelling argument," she said. "Unless we're wildly wrong, however, he would have turned up in life as a crazy person. When I saw him through my gate, he was in pretty rough shape. It would be pretty hard for him to convince anyone of anything in that condition."

He took her empty bottle and set it across from his. "All I'm saying is, if he's not here or here"—he tapped his bottle and then hers—"he might be stuck between the two realms." He tossed an overturned bottle cap between the two bottles. "The only person I know with the skills and position to do such a thing would be Delphine."

Kendell sat next to Cheesecake on the ottoman. "What do you propose doing? Unless we see him strapped to a chair in her office or screaming from the next dimensional room, all she'd have to say is she hasn't seen him. I can't even use the curse like a homing device any longer."

He took one of the bottles and started peeling off the label. At first, she thought it was just the result of nerves, but as he tossed the wads of paper and they ricocheted off the other bottle and onto the table and the bottle cap, she began to wonder what he was thinking.

"You can't use the curse, because we blew up the bank," he said. "And Sere can't enter the Quarter because, in effect, one of our projector's lenses is smashed to smithereens. Those little shards of paranormal glass cover every surface for a ten-block radius, and we're still using the psychometric energy to project our virtual reality into hell."

She wanted to ask him where he was going with his idea, but she didn't want to interrupt his train of thought. He tore more paper until a layer surround the bottle cap.

"In hell, Colin would have experienced the results of our broken equipment like that bottle cap filling up with wads of paper. We were pumping a lot of energy into creating those fake people. With each of them suffering the interference from the old bank, they wouldn't be able to fully absorb the power we're sending. Colin must have had a physical reaction to the extra energy. I'd guess it would be like being around nuclear material. Assuming he did escape hell, he wouldn't be a part of what we're projecting because he hasn't had our enhanced beverages, but he could still be feeling the effects of absorbing our energy. I think we may have dismissed Professor Yates prematurely. It may be a long shot, but if he can prove Colin made it back to life, we'll have something to use on Delphine."

KENDELL TRIED NOT to judge Professor Yates too harshly for the confusing pile of equipment that filled his lab. *Hoarder* wasn't a term often associated with mad scientists, but in his case, the two labels were interchangeable. She wouldn't have cared if it hadn't been for Sere. At least some of the zapping and flashing equipment was responsible for keeping the girl's reproduced body functioning.

Myles looked more comfortable in the chaos. "We think Colin escaped hell, and we know where he would have made the attempt. We don't know when, but it was sometime in the last week. I know your hell diorama only shows the people we're projecting, but has anything odd appeared in that time?"

"You could say that." Professor Yates headed to the wall of electronics that covered one side of the narrow hallway.

"It'll take me a minute to rewind this thing to three days ago. When I say the word, shield your eyes."

Covering a six-foot-long worktable in the old reception office, a three-dimensional projection displayed the whole French Quarter shrouded in a fog of glitter.

"Is this the effect of the bank explosion?" Kendell asked.

"Yep. I've been having a hell of a time stabilizing the projection. That building had so much psychometric energy imbedded in every stone and brick that I'm amazed Myles was even able to set foot inside without being overloaded with people's memories. Once it blew up, all that energy got spread throughout the Quarter like brightly colored sugar on a king cake." The representation of the Quarter reset to late afternoon. "Here we go. Don't look directly at the Quarter. The event will last for a couple of minutes."

When the thin man threw the switch, a bright light appeared in front of Delphine's shop. At first, the flash wasn't too bad, but like a camera bulb going off in slow motion, it grew more intense with every passing second.

Myles was first to turn away. "What the hell?"

The professor kept the display going until the light snapped off. "It was basically a feedback loop like you would get by holding an electric guitar too close to an amplifier. Whatever that was, it was being powered from hell but illuminated in life, so when I projected it from life back into hell, the power kept increasing. I'm guessing you have some idea of what tried to destroy my equipment."

Splotches interfered with Kendell's vision. "That would be Colin."

Myles finished rubbing his eyes. "We were concerned

that once the bank exploded and the virtual people were no longer there to absorb the energy, he might have been bombarded with the current. I guess we were right."

"It would have been nice if you'd given me a heads-up." The professor returned the diorama to its present-time setting.

Kendell didn't want to implicate anyone else in the bombing, but some people, like the professor, needed to know about it. "For everyone's safety, we had to keep the plot a secret."

He emerged from the hallway. His jeans and T-shirt where scorched as if he'd been involved in putting out an electrical fire, and his gray hair stood more on end than usual. "I suppose I should thank you for that, but my ignorance about what was going on with the bank made it difficult to keep this thing operating. As one of the Quarter's oldest buildings, the bank functioned as an indispensable projector. Any word on our little girl?"

Kendell had tried to keep that concern compartmentalized. No one was better able to look after Sere than Sanguine, and she typically didn't want help unless she asked for it. "Sanguine checked in with the band the morning after the explosion. We'd been playing music for Sere all night. She looked fine when she left, but that was over a week ago."

"So long as she doesn't visit the Quarter, she should be okay. I'm doing what I can to stabilize the projection, but until the city gets around to washing down the streets and structures, that psychometric dust will keep messing up my equipment. I hate to think what would happen to

Sere if all the energy we were pumping into her got distorted."

"Do you think Luther might be able to help?" Myles asked. "He is loosely associate with the city. If he were to mention that a thorough cleaning was in order, they might listen."

Professor Yates stroked the week-old stubble on his chin. "Not a bad idea. He wouldn't even have to tell them why. Those who have a clue about what he's up to usually prefer to be kept in the dark about his day-to-day activities. I'll have a talk with him tomorrow."

Kendell wanted to get as much information as possible to avoid having to make another trip to the crumbling office on the wharf. "Any progress on making Sere's body more independent?"

"Her body is still a physical projection," the professor said. "With the bank gone, I'm no longer losing her energy through the seventh gate to Guinee. At least I can now dial in her exact power needs. I'm afraid I've been a little too busy to give much thought to how to make her self-sufficient, though. Some projects don't happen overnight."

"I didn't mean to push. I guess no one's gotten a full night's sleep since the bank explosion. You've been a miracle worker just keeping her alive."

He looked even lankier than usual as he put his hands on the table and leaned over the diorama. "I didn't mean to get snappy, but this little project of yours is becoming a full-time job. If I had the money, I'd hire an assistant."

Kendell looked at all the little people wandering the virtual projection of the make-believe world. "Maybe you could get one of those fake people to help." Her attempt at a joke, however, only made the scientist scratch his head.

"It's not the worst idea. More than a few of those marionettes have gone off script. Usually it happens when one of them is interacting with Colin. I assume it had something to do with Delphine's end of the creation."

Kendell could see that the man's brain had locked onto an idea and he wasn't likely to resurface until he had it all worked out. She turned to Myles and motioned toward the door. "I think we've got what we came for. Time to pay a visit to Delphine."

"Not just yet," Myles said. "I need to stop by the club first. If we're going up against that voodoo priestess and her imprisoned devil, I want my cane with me."

She quietly opened the door while the professor talked to himself about the mathematics involved in giving one of his puppet people independence. Once outside, she took Myles's hand. "Are you sure that's such a good idea? We could be walking into a trap."

He zipped up his coat against the fall chill. "If Colin and Delphine are working together, we're screwed with or without the cane, but it's the only protection we've got."

"And it's the thing Colin most desires."

Myles stood on the sidewalk, facing Frenchmen Street. "I said earlier I was done playing defense against Colin. A weapon is only as good as the one wielding it. We've been trying to keep the cane away from him because we believed he had better mastery of its powers than I do. I no longer believe that's true. The cane obeys me, not him. I'll take my chances."

*I*n spite of what he'd told Kendell, Myles wasn't any happier about the prospect of walking into Delphine's with cane in hand than she was. But if Colin was going to make a play for the powerful stick, Myles wanted to just once have the pleasure of bashing him over the head with it. First, however, he had to retrieve the oversized magic wand.

Charlie's truck had become almost a permanent fixture in front of the club. The beat-up red Ford gave Myles a feeling of calm assurance. "At least someone's watching the business while we go off on these adventures."

Kendell, however, had refused to ride in the beast since the day she'd had to drive it out to the swamp. "Let's just get the cane and go. Every time I enter the club, I feel guilty for not doing enough to keep it running. We really have taken advantage of damn near everyone we know."

"We'll make it up to them once this is over." He pushed open the door so Kendell could enter.

"What brings both my bosses out of their cave in broad daylight?"

Charlie's infectious good humor was one of his most valuable traits. "I need that cane back," Myles said.

"Of course you do," Charlie said from behind the bar. "Eight days cold turkey. I'd say that was a record." He wiped his hands dry on a bar rag. "I've got it out in the truck."

"Are you crazy?" Myles asked. "I said to keep it safe, not haul it around like a jar of olives that fell out of the shopping bag."

Charlie winked as he walked past Myles to the door. "That old jalopy never gets bothered by thieves. It might be the safest hiding place in New Orleans."

"I can attest to that," Kendell said. "Starting that thing was more complex than casting a voodoo spell."

"My old truck can be a little finicky about who she lets operate her controls." Charlie pulled out his keys but didn't head for the cab. Instead, he unlocked and dropped the back gate. It fell to the full extent of its link assemblies with the sound of squealing metal.

Myles wondered if he shouldn't have been a little clearer with Charlie about the wand's dangers, but it was too late to say anything more. "So long as you've still got the cane. Right now, that's all we're worried about."

"You really do sound just like an alcoholic waiting for that first drink after a week on the wagon." He pulled the heavy-gauge wire that hung from the inside of the door where the handle should have been. A loud click sounded from the side. "Just push in the latch of the lift gate, and pull out the side panel."

Myles searched around the mangled edge for something to grab hold of that wouldn't slice into his flesh. He stuck his finger against the thick angled rod and shoved it back into the hole before pulling on the sheet metal. The side of the gate separated to reveal the cane stashed in a shipping tube. "I'm not sure Baron Samedi would approve of the disrespect."

"My understanding was that I should be more worried about how Baron Myles feels about it." After Myles retrieved the cane, Charlie fixed the back of his truck. "Just don't go getting yourself stuck in a situation where I'm unable to help. You hear me?"

Myles patted his friend on the back. "I appreciate it. Don't sweat it if we're not back by opening."

Kendell waited until Charlie returned to the club before dealing with Myles. "So assuming this doesn't go haywire and Colin is in Delphine's shop, what's the plan?"

Myles lifted the cane. "I'm taking him to Guinee. That's the real reason I needed the cane. We've waited as long as we dare, possibly too long. If the loas have their act together and get the new seventh gate up and running, I won't be able to sneak Colin in under their noses. I don't even want to think about the nightmare I'll be facing if that's the case."

"Do you plan on taking me with you?"

He'd been alone in all of the scenarios he'd run. He knew, however, he'd never let her conduct an operation on her own again, so it was only reasonable she'd want to be included. "I'm going to have to be fast and stealthy. Though

I could definitely use the help, I'm afraid two living beings among the dead might attract too much attention."

She frowned. "I didn't really mean that as a question. You're not going without me. If you'll remember, I moved pretty fast during the bank bombing. Taking Colin to Guinee, however, does bring up the other little problem we chose to ignore on our last planning session."

"His death. I haven't forgotten." Myles examined the cane, wondering why neither of its previous owners had thought to hide a saber in the shaft. "We won't know anything for sure about his condition until we talk to Delphine. Oh, and I knew it wasn't a question. I was just trying to give you an out in case you were looking for one. You know I'll never reject your help."

MYLES DIDN'T KNOW what they would find on entering Delphine's shop, but business as usual wasn't it. If she did have Colin tied and gagged somewhere in the building, he had to be under a sleeping spell. They waited around, watching the customers make their purchases. When the latest batch left, smelling of lilacs and absinthe, Myles and Kendell approached Delphine.

As they'd agreed, he let Kendell broach the subject. "We've been to Professor Yates's lab. We know Colin came through the gate and is somewhere in this building. You know I've always seen you as a mentor, but I can't let you side with the devil."

Delphine locked the front door. "If I was working with

Colin, I doubt he'd find his end of our partnership to his liking." She led them to the back room.

Myles tried to take in every square inch without looking overly obvious. "So where is he?"

Delphine pointed at the totem inside the cabinet, which had at one time contained Baron Malveaux. "I killed him. His soul belongs to me. That totem deserves its due, and that debt is the spirit of Archibald Malveaux. Lincoln Laroque knew the risks when he drank the spirit jar, so I have no sympathy for their union known as Colin Malveaux. Marie's soul can rest easy now. She originally prepared the totem knowing the Malveaux spirit needed a suitable cage. I've fulfilled her final unfinished spell."

Kendell stepped back from the statue as if she'd just heard a rattlesnake inside it. "I don't understand why Marie created the voodoo totem but didn't put Baron Malveaux in it herself."

Delphine opened the cabinet and ran her hand over the nail heads as if caressing a child's hair. "Marie Laveau was a seer, but even she couldn't predict the future this far out. Archibald Malveaux did take the cane and become ruler of Guinee. That much she could foresee, and she believed it was her destiny to help him achieve that future. Once he gained power among the loas of the dead, however, she realized her mistake. By then, he was beyond her reach. Though she couldn't see a hundred years into the future, it was her calculation that one day Baron Malveaux would make an attempt to rejoin the living in some fashion. The instructions left with the statue were how I imprisoned him after Myles's possession." She turned to Myles. "That should have satisfied Marie, but I still owed a debt to the Malveaux heirs, including Lincoln Laroque. I'll confess I didn't inherit any abilities as a seer. I had no way of knowing that fool would ingest his ancestor's spirit. Who in their right mind drinks something that smells and tastes like battery acid, rotting flesh, and tar?"

"So that's why you killed him?" Kendell asked.

"It was the only way to drive his soul back into the totem. I've now atoned for my mistake and given Marie the rest she deserved."

Damn you and your voodoo heritage. Myles refrained from starting the fight that had been brewing since the day they'd met. "He belongs in the *deep waters*, not sitting on a shelf like a hunting trophy."

Delphine finally took her hand off of her prized possession. "And you think just because you temporarily disrupted the loas' seventh gate that you can toss this soul in the *deep waters* like a kid skipping a rock across a pond? They'll be waiting for you, and not just the loas you admire. That cane of yours might get you in the door, but once you're bodily in Guinee, every recently dead soul will horn in on you like drunks after a virgin in a brothel. Each member of the dead will see you as their golden ticket out of purgatory—all they have to do is possess your body. And that will include Colin Malveaux. Tell me, how exactly do you intend on keeping him from grabbing the cane and returning to power once he's free of this cage? Convince me, and maybe I'll give him to you, but I'm not letting him fool me the way he fooled Marie Laveau."

Kendell gave Myles the look that said, *She has a point.*

Do I honestly have to do everything? he thought, but he acknowledged that Kendell had endured far worse in her dealings with Colin. "Then help us. Tell me what I have to do. I have the cane. The dead might want to escape, but none of them will cross the person wielding Baron Samedi's staff. Marie Laveau met with me in that totem you treasure and confirmed this stupid stick was always supposed to be mine. Why do you think she did that if not to help me dump Colin into the *deep waters* where he belongs? If we leave him in the totem, how long before the next Malveaux descendant once again tries to reclaim the family's heritage the way Lincoln Laroque did? That totem is a temporary holding cell at best. You're all about revering your ancestor, so go look through her journals and tell me how to get rid of this nemesis to humanity. If she was so mistrustful of Baron Malveaux, she must have had some plan beyond holding his soul captive. Much as I hate to admit it, I need your help."

"And what do I get out of this assistance? I am a businesswoman, and so far, this relationship has been a lot of you two demanding help without offering anything in return."

She was really getting on his nerves, and he couldn't help responding sarcastically. "Do you want me to bring you some trinket from Guinee—a T-shirt maybe?"

"Get me into the World Trade Center. Luther has more than a few items I'd like returned to me."

Like he's ever going to negotiate with you. "I could probably make the introduction. Beyond that, you'd be on your own."

Kendell looked around the room as if she'd lost

something. "I get how you stashed Colin's soul in the totem, but just out of curiosity, where's his body?"

Delphine chewed on her thumbnail. "You don't think I know how to get rid of a corpse with all the swamps around New Orleans? I'm somewhat amazed the police ever find any murder victim." She turned back to Myles. "Okay, I'll help you, but you won't be able to work your way through Guinee and contain Colin at the same time. We can use the totem, but it will need constant monitoring. Only a powerful voodoo practitioner will be able to keep him in his cage. I'll get my bag."

"Not so fast," Kendell said. "I'm the only one going with Myles this time. Show me what I need to do."

THOUGH MYLES HAD HOPED to spare Kendell another life-or-death journey, having her with him sure beat having to make the trip with Delphine. The leather harness the woman tightened around the totem made it look like a dog in need of proper training.

"What happens to the totem when we switch dimensions?" he asked.

Delphine checked the wooden head for any loose or kinked straps. "The sculpture you see now will disappear. Its function in life is to keep a soul supplied with energy and held captive. Once in Guinee, that realm does those things anyway, so the totem becomes redundant. Right now, Colin is like a fish in a bowl. Taking him to the next dimension is like dumping him into a bathtub before he's poured into the ocean of *deep waters.*"

"I get that," Myles said. "What I meant was, what are we going to be dealing with in terms of a crazed devil no longer in his jail cell?"

Delphine shrugged as if the question didn't matter. "Hard to say. Each soul is different."

"What you're really saying is you don't know. Just once, it'd be nice if you didn't try to bluff your way through a problem or pretend it wasn't going to be a big deal."

Kendell wrapped one of the leather ends of the harness around her hands and tested the weight. "None of that matters at this point. We have what we're after. Where do you want to make our entrance to Guinee?"

"Not here." The old voodoo shop was the last place in life he might see, but the fact that he hated it wasn't what made him hesitate. "We need someplace discreet. I don't want to materialize in the middle of Afterlife Street. If Baron Samedi's gate is closed for repairs, who knows how many people will be wandering around lost."

"Sounds like Mardi Gras in the Quarter," Kendell said.

"That's what I'm afraid of, especially if that rabid dog in the voodoo handbag decides to get frisky." Being in the voodoo lair affected his thinking too much for him to trust his conclusions. Though he distrusted Delphine, he hoped she knew at least something about the objects in her care. "Do you think it's safe to bring that thing back to our apartment?"

The voodoo practitioner straightened up her office. "So long as you're in life, that totem is perfectly stable."

Right. And Lincoln Laroque drinking from the spirit jar should have just given him indigestion. But continuing the animosity would only further delay their trip to Guinee to get rid of Colin Malveaux.

"The dogs might object," Kendell said, "but any paranormal location could open a door back to Sanguine and Sere if Colin were to escape our grasp. If this goes wrong, I don't want them at risk."

They left the shop with Myles holding the cane with its glowing green crystal and Kendell carrying the voodoo totem with both hands. He wondered how much attention they'd get on the short walk home. "Good thing it's Halloween season. We probably won't even be the strangest-looking couple in the Quarter."

She hefted the head up to her abdomen. "So long as no one asks to pet our wooden demon."

As always, the dogs came rushing off the ottoman when Myles opened the door, but both pups stopped well short of Kendell and growled ominously at the voodoo totem in his hands. He set the cane against the wall and bent down to Cheesecake and Doughnut Hole. "It's okay. I know you hate these things. I'll tell you secret: I do too. Kendell and I are going to dump this thing in the afterlife, and you'll never have to see it again. Deal?"

The dogs circled away from Kendell, but at least they stopped growling.

Myles could see the pain in her eyes. "The dogs love you. It's just the stupid totem."

"I know, but I've never returned home to Cheesecake's animosity. She's always so happy to see me."

Myles got off the floor and snatched his cane. "Then the sooner we get rid of that hideous thing, the sooner we can get back to the lives we love."

Though Guinee didn't mirror the French Quarter the way Agnes's hell did, some truths remained between dimensions. Myles knew if they left a building to make the crossover, they would materialize outside in Guinee, and walking from one room to the next in life would mean they would remain inside a structure in death. With the potential of so many people wandering the streets, he figured the doorway from the hallway to the bathroom would be the safest bet. He put his arm around Kendell's waist so she could maintain control of Colin with both hands. "No matter what happens, keep hold of Colin. I'll do my best to land us someplace safe."

She snuggled close to his side. "Then what?"

"I don't know. We're going to have to find an access to the *deep waters* on our own. While you were helping Delphine cast her binding spells from Marie's diary, did you happen to see any hints about what we'll be dealing with once Colin is free of his cage?"

Kendell set the totem on the floor so she could reposition her hold on the straps. "My best guess is I'll be holding a bound wild creature. Delphine said we shouldn't even refer to him by name in case anyone is listening in, so I'm guessing he might not even look human."

He looked around the totem for a second handhold. "Colin wasn't a small man in life. Do you want me to hold the totem in case he's even bigger in death?"

She hefted the wooden head back to her waist. "We're

talking about the difference of mass verses energy. Right now, he's a decent weight, but there are no real bodies in Guinee, just spirits."

"You're missing the point."

She shook her head. "I'm not. You're offering to be chivalrous by handling the totem for me, but whatever he is on the other side, it's my job to contain him. My spells will work like the muscles of my arms. I'll be okay."

"If we ever have to deal with voodoo again in the future, I'm relying on you to find the answers. Delphine's ideas never end up being that encouraging." He cleared his thoughts of people and focused on the emptiest space he could imagine. *Just me, Kendell, and the devil.*

With his eyes closed, Myles led Kendell into the bathroom. When he opened them, they were standing in a dark broom closet. The smell of putrid water was quickly overcome with that of rotting flesh.

Kendell used both hands to hold the wild animal bound in chains. "This is not what I expected. I swear he's about to break free."

Myles took one of the leads that were jangling off the beast and yanked hard. "Looks like it'll take both of us to keep him restrained after all. This is not going to make us inconspicuous."

The beast writhing against its bonds didn't appear even remotely human. Its contortions, screams, and smell put to shame the Church's descriptions of the damned in hell.

Kendell retreated to a wall of the closet. "We can't possibly find the *deep waters* if we're both wrestling this creature."

Myles grabbed his walking stick and aimed the green stone at the writhing spirit. "Settle down, or this cane is going to pierce your soul."

The screaming stopped, though without the distraction of noise, Myles's nose recoiled from the smell. *It's as if every misdeed this guy ever committed became leftovers in a refrigerator abandoned after a hurricane. The smell is indescribable.* From Kendell's watering eyes and the way she held her hand over her nose, he figured she didn't need to hear his observations about the odor.

"I feel like the stink is creeping up my arms," she said.

He needed someplace to connect to the *deep waters*, but he couldn't leave Kendell alone with the beast. The room was small, but Myles thought by moving some buckets around, he might be able to lie flat on the floor. "If you think you can control him, I'm going to lie down and see if I can connect to the *deep waters*. Maybe then I'll see a portal."

"Whatever you come up with, do it fast. I don't think I can stand being in this stinky broom closet much longer."

Myles hunched down to the floor, praying nothing he smelled or touched was contagious. "Hopefully, the *deep waters* aren't actually a cesspool." Kendell corralled the beast to the far corner of the room, but having it still tower over Myles wasn't that conducive to achieving inner peace.

"Right now," Kendell said, "I'd be happy to toss him into the nearest toilet and pull the handle in the hopes that it would eventually dump into the sea of humanity."

Myles was tempted to agree, but any possibility of Colin's escape had to be avoided at all cost. "Just give me a couple of minutes, and I'll figure a way out of this mess."

For being so close to the source of all human spirits, Myles found the attempted connection surprisingly difficult. He grabbed the cane to have something to focus on for his psychometric journey. Like downing a glass of water on a hot day only to discover it was actually vodka, being in contact with the sum of all human energy knocked him into another state of awareness.

Kendell kicked the cane out of his hands. "Are you okay? You started convulsing worse than our beast."

Myles struggled to get to his hands and knees. "I think I just experienced the full power of the cane. It's not what it can do but what it connects to. I thought it was only useful for traveling between dimensions, but that's just a side effect of being in touch with every human soul, living and dead."

She was still trying to contain the monster against the wall. "And you're sure you're okay after that?"

He worked his way to his feet. "The link only lasted a moment. Much longer, and I might not have found my way back. The *deep waters* are underneath all of Guinee. It looked like a subterranean ocean with waterfalls feeding into it. I only got a glimpse. You can't imagine how beautiful it was."

She still looked worried. "So long as there weren't turds floating in the water. Do you think one of those waterfalls is the seventh gate?"

"Sounds right, but we're going to have to get down there ourselves. I won't fully accept that we've fulfilled our mission until I see this beast become one with the water."

"So we have to leave this cozy little room?" she asked. "Damn. And I was just getting used to the smell."

He snatched the cane and aimed it at the door. It opened to a hallway balcony overlooking a loud old-fashioned bar and gaming tables. "We have to get to the basement."

"Without being seen? Maybe we could wait until closing. This creature isn't going to be quiet once we leave this room."

Myles was done trying to be subtle. "This place never closes. As for the loas, they don't matter." He turned back to her. "I've seen things with this cane. We have the power of life behind us. Everything is going to work out fine."

"You realize who you sound like right now?" She held up the heavy-gauge metal chain.

"He found the wrong answers. Our plan is different. Instead of being in charge of events like a sorcerer manipulating the future, we're going to rely on the cumulative desire of human hope to shield us."

She pulled on her section of chain with both hands to get the beast to move. "You're not making a lot of sense, but I'll follow where you lead."

He wanted to explain what he'd seen, but words failed to describe the certainty he felt. "Give me one of those ends of chain, and I'll help keep hold of our creature."

He turned left into the hallway just as the last person headed down the stairs at the far end. The sounds of drinking, singing, and shouting indicated the customers below were too busy with their own affairs to pay much attention to anything else. Myles didn't bother hanging close to the shadows but turned down the stairs, hammering his cane on each landing with one hand and yanking on the chain to the beast with the other.

"You don't think we should be a *little* more inconspicuous?" Kendell brought up the rear. Her cautious movements were slowing down the procession.

"I don't give a damn who notices, but no one will. You'll see." At the bottom of the stairs, Myles turned in to the kitchen, still tugging on the chain like a dog owner expecting the animal to heel.

"How do we get to the basement?" She was whispering, not realizing she didn't need to.

He pointed the cane at the back door. "There's an outside entrance to a root cellar. That's as low as we can go in this building. There's a grotto of the *deep waters* that extends under this side of the street, so all we'll need to do is punch our way down."

"And what if we run into one of the loas? They must have some kind of a security system against people just directly accessing the *deep waters*." Her whisper was so quiet on the last words that he barely heard her.

"They're all busy figuring out what to do with the backlog of souls. Those waterfalls I saw were mere trickles compared to the influx of the dead. Right now, we're the least of their worries."

She was still lagging behind. "Aren't we going to need shovels?"

He held up the cane. "We've got everything we need. Now, get a move on. I'd like to get home before the dogs miss their dinner."

Outside of the saloon, the cane guided Myles to the locked doors that tilted back toward the building. Though the alleyway was vacant, the crush of revelers on the street threatened to spill into the empty space. With no one looking, Myles aimed the green crystal at the lock, which snapped open.

"Cool trick. Too bad the doors didn't magically open as well." Kendell huddled against the wall. Her position indicated she wanted to keep as much distance from Colin as possible while also trying to be invisible.

"We'll be out of sight in just a minute." He set the cane against the wall so he could maintain his hold on Colin and pull the doors open with his free hand. Every second that the cane wasn't in his hand left him with a growing feeling of anxiety.

With the access open, he retrieved his stick and instantly knew there was nothing to worry about. But they had to keep moving. He followed Kendell and the beast down the small ladder and pulled the doors closed behind them. Only the green glow from his cane illuminated the dirt-sided cellar.

"Hold onto his leash." With his hands free of the chain, Myles turned the cane over and hit the dirt floor with the crystal.

Like shattering ice, the ground collapsed around them, but instead of freefalling to their doom, they floated down like leaves on a windless afternoon. When they landed, they stood on a rock outcropping surrounded by an endless ocean.

Myles stood over the writhing body. "Take off his chains."

"Are you sure that's a good idea? Couldn't we just kick him into the water?"

He aimed the crystal at the beast to quiet him down. "It doesn't work that way. He needs to become one with all humanity. That's one of the things I learned while holding the cane. I've floated on these waters many times but never bonded with it. Moving on to the *deep waters* isn't just about dying. It's a matter of accepting that we're each only a small part of a much greater whole. Dying frees us from our bodies, but letting go of our souls has to be a conscious decision."

He kept the cane aimed at Colin while Kendell carefully unlocked the chains. Once freed, the beast unfolded its bloated body and stretched out on spindly legs to its full nine-foot height. Its skin was covered in boils and scars. The contortions that rippled its wolflike face exuded pure contempt. Nothing about the body looked human except its basic structure. It extended its bony hand toward the cane. "Give it to me."

Myles didn't back down. "So now we see your true self. Welcome to my version of the seventh gate. Instead of requiring you to accept the *deep waters* like Baron Samedi, I give you a choice: enter the reservoir of human souls as an outcast to be forever condemned—drowning for an eternity in humanity's judgment—or embrace the love that has occasionally found a home in your spirit and let your life go. Either way, you're not getting out of this grotto." He pushed the crystal against the beast's chest.

The animal's howl gave way to the outcries of a man. "What am I supposed to do?"

Myles pushed the stone farther into the man-beast's chest. "The time for your education is over."

A beating heart appeared under the green glow of the crystal. "Serephine." As Colin fell backward into the *deep waters*, the beast that had driven his existence faded away, leaving only the man. Instead of submerging himself in the waves, he melded into the lapping ocean. The last Myles saw of Colin Malveaux were the sky-blue eyes that turned one final time to Kendell and the smile that ensued.

Kendell stood at the shore between life and death. "Rest in peace."

Myles watched the waters to make sure Colin didn't have one last trick up his sleeve. The calm ocean reflected the rock cave like glass. Without realizing what he was doing, Myles kicked off his shoe and dipped his toe in the welcoming liquid.

"What are you doing?" The panic in Kendell's voice was like a lifeguard trying to yank him out of a pool.

"All my life, people have told me I was crazy for thinking I could read energy in objects. You were the only one who believed in me, even when I doubted myself." He looked at her and waved at the water. "This is it. Everything I've believed about life from the time I could think. It's right here." The desire to dive in made him feel as if his clothing would fall right off his body.

"You're not leaving me. This is not your death. We've done what we came to do. It's time we left before the loas figure out we're here."

He slipped his foot, from toes to ankle, into the calm love of all human souls. The temperature and texture made it hard to know where his flesh ended and the water began.

I could finally slip away into what I've always dreamed of finding.

She grabbed his arm and wrenched him so forcefully back onto the rock outcropping that he landed on his face. "Knock it off right now." Her voice was faltering. She sounded far away even though he could still feel her hand on his arm.

As with the welcoming water, he wasn't sure where her fingers ended and his forearm began. He didn't just love her. She was a physical part of him—at least in the spirit world.

"Come with me," he said.

"You're acting like a damn fool. We've got an entire life ahead of us and two dogs that need us. When the time is right, many years from now, we'll come back here, and I'll gladly go for a swim with you. But right now, we still have things to do."

He turned back to the ocean of souls with tears in his eyes. As they ran down his cheeks, he knew his sorrow would join with the *deep waters*. "You're right. I don't know what came over me." He reached for the cane that connected him to the place beyond the shore, but instead of being drawn forward, he stayed huddled on the rocks like someone afraid of falling off a ledge.

She eased off of her viselike hold of his arm. "You got a glimpse of the sum of human love. Who wouldn't be enticed by something like that? I know I can't compare to that, but I need you with me."

He turned to look at her. Tears were flowing down her face too. "You are my *deep waters*—at least, the precious glass of it that I get to keep with me in life. I'm sorry I scared you.

Let's go home. The dogs are probably missing us." He slipped the shoe back onto his foot as if it were his protection from the siren calls of the deep. As he got up and took her hand, he took one last longing look at the vast expanse of water. For the only time in his encounters with Colin Malveaux, he actually envied the man.

For the first time in what felt like years, Kendell woke up without the feeling that the world was her responsibility to save. She rolled against Myles's back and wrapped her arm tightly around his chest. Though sex had always been an exhilarating experience, she'd never before understood what people meant by the term *making love*. In the past, it had always sounded so fake—as if people were trying to cover the raunchy act in a cloak of respectability. She nuzzled her cheek against his shoulder. "There just aren't any words to describe last night."

He turned over to face her. His cheeks and eyes were still pink from the emotions that had been released. "We were like two halves of the same spirit." He frowned. "You're right. There are no words."

She pressed her head to his chest. "I can't believe how close I came to losing you yesterday. Don't ever scare me like that again. Understand?"

He ran his fingers through her hair from the top of her head to her back. "I'd like to say I don't know what came over me, but that would be a lie. The only other time I've felt like that was in your arms." Though his fingers stopped at the end of her hair, the tingling continued down to her toes.

She undulated against his body. "I like that."

"My touch, or that you make me feel wanted?"

"Both," she said. "If I wasn't having a craving for coffee, I'd recommend we stay in each other's arms all day."

He took the hint and kissed her on the head. "Stay here. I'll go make it."

Cheesecake stretched out in the warm indentation left by Myles. Doughnut Hole lay curled up at the foot of the bed. Kendell snuggled deeper under the heavy comforter while she waited for him to bring her a cup. The feeling of family harmony had her humming "Here Comes the Sun."

"Somebody's in an awfully good mood. I'm not so confident in my moves as to believe this is strictly about our night of passion." Myles handed her the cup of coffee and rejoined her in bed. Cheesecake gave him a grumpy look at being moved but didn't outwardly protest.

"I feel like it's the first day of summer vacation, or maybe the day after graduation. I still find it hard to believe we actually defeated that devil."

He tickled Doughnut Hole with his feet, enticing the dog to join the family. "You're not worried life will feel somewhat boring now that you just have to run a business and play with the band?"

"Not even a little bit. When one adventure ends, there's

always another on the horizon. Hopefully, the next one will be something more positive than defeating evil."

He contemplated his coffee. "And what about Sanguine?"

Stop trying to cast a shadow on my happy morning, Kendell thought, but she knew he was only trying to help air out any lingering issues. "Of course, I'd rather she returned to life, but she'll never leave hell until Sere can as well. Until we find a way to make Sere's body real, that girl is going to need someone to raise her. At least without Colin driving our need to make hell a realm of the damned, Sanguine can turn it into a world fit for a growing child. We do still have our gates, so it's not like we'll never hear from them again."

He set his cup on the nightstand and snuggled back against her. "Hopefully, she'll check in soon."

The small black puppy circled around the covers until he made himself into a fluffy ball pressed against Myles's side.

"And what about you and the loas of the dead?" she asked. "You do still have that cane."

"I'm sure they'll make contact soon. I'm hoping we dropped Colin off in such a way that they'll believe it was Sere and stop their search for her."

Between the coffee, comforter, dogs, and Myles's love, Kendell felt warm all over. "I guess Sanguine can't be the only one looking out for the child. We'll probably always have to run interference from our reality. If the loas figure out it wasn't her soul we dropped into the *deep waters*, they'll be coming after all of us."

"I'm positive Papa Ghede will be hitting me up sooner or later with another interdimensional problem. With our proximity to Sere, we'll have to be careful dealing with the loas of the dead. Our advantage, however, is that those spirits will owe me, and we can keep an eye out for any time they might be getting suspicious."

She reached over and fluffed up the little dog's head. "At least we got this puppy out of the deal."

"And the deed to the club."

She laughed. "Right, and that. I suppose I should be grateful to never have to work for someone else again, but honestly, I'm more excited about the puppy. I'm just glad we got to share the wealth with Polly and Lynn. I suppose I should think of something nice to do for Scraper and Minerva now that this is all over."

"If we're going to try to pay back all the people who've helped us, I'm not sure where we'd stop. I'm guessing gratitude is going to be a lifelong condition for us."

Kendell snuggled down in the covers and pulled Cheesecake onto her stomach. "And you, little dog, have been my savior more times than I can count. I love you so much."

The dog started kissing Kendell's face with such enthusiasm that the licking felt like a tongue facial.

～

THOUGH MYLES SHARED in Kendell's sense of relief, he still had the burden of the loas hovering over him. At any moment, they might show up and demand he risk his very soul for some fool mission again. So when she headed off to band practice, he snagged the bottle of expensive rum from the cupboard and went out to the veranda for a late-afternoon shot.

Papa Ghede was already sitting at the metal table with an empty glass in hand. "I thought you might want to chat."

Of course you did. Myles filled the loa's glass before doing the same with his own. "How are things in Guinee?"

"We'll have the seventh gate back up and running by the end of the week. A hole was discovered under one of the saloons, and the *deep waters* are a soul fuller than expected. You wouldn't happen to know anything about that, would you?"

Myles doubted there was much point in lying, but hopefully, a little redaction of the truth wouldn't be noticed. "I couldn't exactly turn a soul that had been torn through multiple dimensional shifts loose in Guinee. You already had your hands full."

Papa Ghede shook his head while contemplating the rum in his glass. "No need to explain. I appreciate the help. So long as the tally of the living and the dead remains constant, how we get to the balance is of only marginal concern. Now, if that soul you have locked in hell were to break loose into life, we'd need to hear about it. I hope you understand."

Is this a warning or a threat? "We have control of the situation."

"Then we can consider this commission complete."

Myles watched the dogs lounging inside the apartment in a patch of sunlight. "Not quite. There is the matter of payment for services rendered. What I want has to do with

Cheesecake and her pups. I don't ever want any of their human companions to suffer a loss of their beloved dog."

The old loa's smile revealed ivory-colored teeth coated in rum. "The souls of those animals are bonded to the spirits of the people who care for them. Neither will continue without the other."

Why can't you just speak in plain English? "So when it comes my time to die, Doughnut Hole will join me? But he won't die before that?"

"Isn't that what I just said?"

Myles needed another drink. With no life-or-death challenge on the horizon, he filled his glass to the rim. *I haven't had a proper hangover in months.* "Just making sure. The terms of our arrangement aren't always as clear as I'd like. Speaking of which, how do we go forward?"

"As I said when I gave you the cane, we will have jobs for you from time to time. Right now, the balance between our worlds doesn't require an intervention among the living."

I'll bet your realm is a mess, though. Myles kept his observations to himself. He didn't even want to imply any willingness on his part to help police Guinee. "Then I'm free to live my life again?"

"For the time being."

KENDELL COULDN'T REMEMBER a gig where she'd been so excited to be onstage. Her music was her own again. Any magic that ensued from her guitar was strictly to enhance the crowd's enjoyment. She was Olympia Stain, lead guitarist for Polly Urethane and the Strippers. No devil would walk through the door on this night. No souls would need her music to find their way home. And her band was rocking out in full force.

Behind the bar, Myles and Charlie once again flipped bottles between them in time to the music. All the customers were up on their feet, singing, laughing, and dancing. Kendell laid into a riff, knowing the enhanced energy that filled the room would be pumped into the mirror club in hell. Even if Sere was too young to frequent the dance club and Sanguine too occupied with the child for a night out, the energy had to have a positive influence on the realm.

Kendell didn't set her guitar down until the last group of customers stumbled their way to the door at two in the morning. Even then, she wished she could continue playing instead of closing up the club. "That was some night."

Polly handed her a bottle of water. "Girl, you played like there was no tomorrow. I don't know how you're going to find the energy for our next gig. Our regulars are going to start expecting a whole new level of commitment from all of us. Way to set the bar higher than it already was."

Kendell meekly shrugged. "What use is being onstage if we don't stretch our abilities from time to time?"

Polly tapped her foot on the plywood stage as if the limb had fallen asleep. "Anyone else feel that vibration?"

Kendell didn't feel a thing, but the other bandmates nodded their agreement with Polly. Myles came out from behind the bar. "Someone's calling us from the beyond. I can feel it from the speakeasy as well. Looks like maybe Sanguine has come out of hiding."

Everyone cleared off the stage so Polly could draw the veve. Sanguine showed up with her hand on Sere's shoulder. "Did I get my timing right?"

Kendell stood as close to the stage as she could. She desperately wished she could hold them both in her arms. "Were you intentionally avoiding us?"

Sanguine caressed the girl's short strawberry-blond hair. "I knew what was about to happen. Seemed like a good time for the two of us to take a little flying road trip."

Lynn knelt down on the floor to put herself at Sere's level. "Did you have a good time?"

"I've never met so much wildlife. Sangy introduced me to turtles and pelicans and snakes, but the alligators were my favorite. She says we're going to spend years just getting to know every wild animal we can find."

"Sounds magical," Lynn said.

Sanguine leaned over and kissed Sere on the head. "Why don't you stay here and tell the band all about our adventure. Kendell, Myles, and I are going to go out back for an adult conversation."

"Okay, Sangy." The girl's trusting smile made Kendell's heart ache.

Myles rushed out back to set up the speakeasy but not before Kendell caught the glint of tears in his eyes. *You're going to make a great father, whether you know it or not.* She waited until Sanguine had left before finally turning away from Sere and her animated telling of her swamp experience.

Once the three of them were out in the courtyard, Kendell thought Sanguine looked more relaxed than she ever remembered. "Mind telling me what that absence was all about? And don't give me that *I was protecting Sere* bullshit."

Sanguine flapped her wings then rubbed them together as if they'd had an intense workout. "I never could hide much from you. I took a little trip into the future to figure out what to do about Sere. The challenge with those voyages is that if I want them to come true, I have to be very precise in my actions. One little misstep, unintended encouragement, or outburst, and my hoped-for result will go off the rails. Sending Colin into the *deep waters* required a very well-defined chain of actions. I saw that you and Myles had everything under control, but if I let on about anything I'd seen, I might distract you from Colin's fate."

Kendell thought the explanation sounded a little too rehearsed. "And what do you see now?"

Sanguine looked toward the club and the sound of Sere's lively recounting of their adventure. "I'm staying to raise Sere, but you already knew that. I won't be doing it alone, however. These gates will take on a whole new purpose. I'm going to need all of you to help raise that child, and my first request might be a little unexpected. I'd like to start Sere on a physical exercise program. Do you think you could convince Joe Cazenave to stop by the speakeasy? This courtyard would make a wonderful workout arena. Our schedule is open, so whenever is convenient for him will work for us."

Kendell could hear Sere getting even more amped up in

the next room. "I guess she does have a lot of child-driven energy. Do we need to talk to Professor Yates about an interdimensional sedative?"

Sanguine didn't laugh at what Kendell had meant as a joke. "No, Sere is exactly how she needs to be, but that energy does require focus. Joe has the perfect set of skills, but he doesn't come across as a kid person. Approach him gently, but let him know it's important to me."

Myles sat in a metal chair with his feet up on the table while enjoying a beer. "And what can we offer?"

Sanguine's smile had a maturity that Kendell didn't remember being there before her voyage of future discovery. "You each have your skills, so I want Sere to have time with all of you, but the most important part of her education is just being around other people. This dimension will forever be populated by doppelgängers. My fear is that she'll grow up to see people as nothing more than dolls without souls. I can't let that happen, and as I'm no longer entirely human, Sere is going to need some better role models."

Myles took his feet off the table. "You flew into the future, so you must know the answer to my next question. Are you two ever leaving hell?"

"I've learned my lesson about predicting too much. I only went far enough to discover what best to do about Sere when it came to her father."

Kendell knew her friend was lying, but Sanguine never hid anything important without good reason. "So we'll treat Sere as if one day she will leave the make-believe realm and join the living. Between the lot of us, I'm sure we can provide an adequate homeschooling. The band and I will start doing some research on curriculums. I'm sure they'll be more than happy to help." Kendell stared Sanguine straight in the eye. "And what about you? Surely, you'll need more adult interactions than we can provide."

Sanguine flapped her wings like a bird airing out her feathers. "I gave romance a try. I'm not sure I won't miss it, but looking after Sere feels like enough meaning for this lifetime. If I get too horny, I can always get my needs met the way Colin did, though I'll probably avoid the back alleys."

Kendell hated the idea of her friend being destined to such a lonely life. "But if we assume Sere will one day cross over, why can't we do the same for you? I realize interdimensional dating would take online relationships to a whole new level, but we can introduce you to people."

Sanguine spread out her wings. "And you just expect me to sit here flirting with someone over this communication link while keeping these things tucked behind me? I'm afraid I'll never find a way of keeping them from betraying every one of my emotions. I appreciate the offer. I'm sure we'll have plenty of time to discuss my love life. For now, though, I'm happy to focus my energy on Sere."

"I'll talk to Professor Yates about how to make Sere self-sufficient," Myles said. "That would have to be the first step in allowing her to cross over. These things have to be planned. We'll find a way of rescuing you both."

Sanguine smiled and shook her head. "You're not getting it. I'm happy to be Sere's surrogate mother. Even if you did manage to let her into life, she'd never be fully human, just as I'm not. You can't lay that kind of a trip on a young girl. Maybe when she's an adult, we can discuss her leaving this realm, but for now, the best thing you can do is help me raise her."

~

SANGUINE TOOK Sere by the hand and left the club. Though there wasn't much in the alternate world to fear, Kendell was right. Sere needed to be raised with an eye toward crossing over to the world filled with people. But for the moment, they could enjoy a walk through the busy music-club district in the middle of the night without a concern in the world.

"I guess we should find a place to stay. I can't keep flying you in from the swamp every time we need to talk to real people."

"I like the swamp. Why can't we just use your gate when you need your adult talks?"

If it were up to Sanguine, isolation wouldn't be an issue. But Sere deserved better. "The gates aren't just for my use. There are people on the other side who want to be a part of your life too. You and I will have our special time in the swamp, but you need more than I can give you. A person's growth is in part the result of those around them. I also want you to have some independence. Maybe not just yet, but eventually, you're going to want to do things on your own. The swamp is a long way from New Orleans." She nodded at all the people dancing in the clubs, flirting on the street, and enjoying life to the fullest. "I know you don't feel like you fit in. Some of us never do, even when we are in the realm of the living. Getting to know these doppelgängers will be good practice for when we do cross out of hell." *I have to keep that goal in mind.*

"I like it when you fly me. If we stay here, will you still give me lifts?"

Sanguine resisted the urge to swoop Sere up in her arms and go for a flight over the river in the light of the full moon. "Of course I will. We'll go flying all the time. Just like on our little camping trip. And we'll sleep outside under the stars and talk to animals, and I'll teach you all about how life works. But while we're in town, we need a place to stay. That's what people do."

Sere pointed to a group of homeless teenagers who were singing for tips. "They get to stay outside."

Sanguine could see this wasn't going to be an argument she could win. Hypocrisy had a way of biting her in the ass. "The truth is, I spent most of my childhood sleeping outside in a hammock on my grandmother's porch. But wouldn't you want a place to keep your stuff? What about when it rains?"

"I don't like stuff. It's hard to hold onto when you're flying me around. And I'm sure Auntie Kendell would let us sleep in the club when it rains."

Sanguine spread her wings protectively over Sere. "I'm sure there will be times when we'll hang out in the club talking to Kendell, Myles, and the band all night, but tonight, I have to find a place for you to rest your head. It's very late, and you need some sleep."

"Why don't we just sleep there?" Sere pointed to a house with a For Sale sign tacked to the fence.

It had been a long day, and though Sanguine wasn't a fan of breaking and entering, it wasn't as if the place was actually inhabited in their realm. "I suppose it wouldn't hurt for the night, so long as we don't get into the habit of just taking what we want. That would be wrong."

"Why?"

Raising you to understand people while living in a world without consequences is going to be a lot harder than I thought.

BOOK LIST

<u>Technopia Series:</u>
(writing as Greg Chase)
Creation
Evolution
Damnation
Salvation

<u>The Malveaux Curse Mysteries :</u>
(writing as G.A. Chase)
Dog Days of Voodoo
You, Me, and the Voodoo Queen
Oops! I Voodooed Again
Voodoo You Love
Voodoo You Think You Are
Look What You Made Me Voodoo
Love Me Like Voodoo

<u>The Devil's Daughter:</u>
(writing as G.A. Chase)
Hell in a Head Gasket

<u>Other Stories</u>
Through the Lens

ABOUT THE AUTHOR

G.A. Chase is the pen name for Greg Chase. He is a science fiction and paranormal author living in New Orleans with his wife, fellow author Deanna Chase, and their two shih tzu dogs. On any given day you can find him behind his computer, people watching in the quarter, or out in his studio creating stories in glass. His glass work can be found at www.chase-designs.com.

www.gregchaseauthor.com